ONE FOR SORROW

All his life Steven Fenn had wanted
to be a farmer. At last, when his
wife died and his children were grown
up and had left home, he was able
to fulfil his ambition by becoming
the owner of Hollow End Farm in the
village of Salem Hardacre.

Everything went well. He built up
the herd, he was well served by old
Joey and Sarah Harden – there had
been Hardens working at Hollow
End for generations – and he was
soon accepted into the friendly,
peaceful community of the village, a
community which included the young
artist Mark Tilley and his wife Sue,
and Robbie Preston, the hardbitten,
cynical newspaperman.

The first rumours of an epidemic
of foot-and-mouth disease cause
barely a ripple in Salem Hardacre,
but before long the terrible scourge
has spread to the neighbouring
countryside, and Steven and his
friends face the destruction of all
that they have lived and worked for.

One for Sorrow is no sentimental,
idealised picture of rural England,
but a tense, realistic and very moving
novel. If there is perhaps a streak of
bitterness, it is redeemed by Joyce
Stranger's great compassion.

Joyce Stranger

One For Sorrow

CORGI BOOKS
A DIVISION OF TRANSWORLD PUBLISHERS LTD

ONE FOR SORROW

A CORGI BOOK 552 10127 3

First publication in Great Britain

PRINTING HISTORY
Corgi edition published 1969
Corgi edition reprinted 1973
Corgi edition reissued 1976
Corgi edition reprinted 1980

Copyright © 1969 by Joyce Stranger

This book is set in 10pt. Times

Corgi Books are published by
Transworld Publishers Ltd.,
Century House, 61–63 Uxbridge Road,
Ealing, London W5 5SA

Set printed and bound in Great Britain by
Cox & Wyman Ltd., Reading

One For Sorrow

NOBODY who lives in a farming area is likely to forget 1967.

The foot and mouth epidemic that wiped out a large part of the Cheshire population of farm animals was one of the worst ever recorded.

I had friends who had lived on edge for weeks; speaking to them on the telephone was a sharp translation into another world, a world that no one would wish to share.

This story grew as the result of many conversations, with farmers, with vets, and with my own friends. I have not tried to criticize in any way the policies laid down, but I have tried to show just how various people react to them. There are always two sides to every question and sometimes more than two.

I am not competent to judge, and have not attempted to do so. The slaughter policy probably upsets the town population more than it does the farmers, many of whom feel it is the only satisfactory treatment, much as they dislike it. They are used to their beasts being killed, but not to utter waste. Sheep find their way to market, not, under normal conditions, to the slaughter pits.

Farmers cannot afford sentimentality, but this does not mean that they are devoid of feeling, which is a very different thing. There are always animals that have some extra endearing trait, and often these remain, in spite of the fact that they ought to have been slaughtered years before. There are unfeeling farmers, but I have not met any, and I have met dozens.

I knew a cow called Mollie, who was twenty, and who be-

7

haved like the cow Shala in my story. She died last year, having been kept on as a pet long after her usefulness was ended.

I know a farmer whose dog always sleeps at the foot of his bed, and is a pet dog, as opposed to the working dogs who belong outside. I know of farms where bottle-fed lambs roam in the yard, because no one has the heart to consign them to their more usual fate.

I once saw a farmer with a cine camera filming the contract men who were shearing his sheep. He patted each beast as it left the shearers, and his dog could not bear him out of its sight.

It is easy to think that because rearing beasts for market is a business, they do not care. They do. I remember one man, who is now dead, who came every night and sat in his car and smoked his pipe and watched the cattle in his fields. If ever a man looked as if he had achieved his heart's desire, that man did. He had started farming very late in life, and found it good.

My book is dedicated to my many farming friends, and it is also dedicated to all those farmers who lost their beasts in the epidemic, with the hope that they now have cattle in their yards, and have been able to recover their losses. Though for those who had herds with longstanding pedigrees things will never be quite the same again.

Cheshire.
October 1967–
January 1968.

CHAPTER ONE

THE hare crouched in her form, long ears listening. Autumn fogged the low hills. Bracken, browned and dying, slimed at the roots, masked her view, but she knew the lie of the land as well as she knew her own two forepaws. She needed to know it, for a daily chase from the fox was a familiar event. Her long legs took her swiftly up the hill, her cunning showed her how to double on her trail, how to mask her scent by leaping the running beck and landing in marshy ground, how to leap sideways and race again, leaving the fox bewildered. He never learned, having hopes that, one day, he would feast on the lolloping hare and not have to turn hungrily to mice and rats that abounded near the farms.

It was a damp morning. The hare did not move. Her bold brown eyes watched, but her nose and ears told her of more than she could see. Beyond the slope of the hill there were new scents borne on the wind; scents that she remembered from the year before. There were sounds, too. The eager excited voices of men, the music of hounds, the mill and turmoil and ferment of the beagle hunt. Her body tensed. She knew they would be on her trail, that the hounds would find her trace and she would have to run for her life, a ploy that did not bother her unduly. She had run often before, and her skill had ensured that she would run again.

She waited, seemingly unafraid. She was swift and strong and so fearless that, only a few days ago, she had turned in her tracks and sent a lone chasing mongrel dog rolling paws over head as hind legs kicked him ferociously. Before he had recovered from astonishment she was over the brow of the hill.

Outside the Grey Goose the beagles waited for orders. The Master looked over the followers, who were congregating in small groups. He knew the regulars and nodded at them. They could be relied on to obey the rules, to shut gates, to respect walls and hedges, and keep off land under cultivation. They would stay out of the way of the hounds, and refrain from heading the hare. He did not have to worry about them. But there was a group of lads at the end of the lane, jostling one another, joking, laughing raucously, pushing with thigh and shoulder, aiming to impress the girls. He knew none of them and frowned. It only needed two or three hooligans to spoil a whole day's sport.

'Told you you'd find all sorts here,' Mark Tilley remarked to Steven Fenn who farmed at Hollow End under Eagle Hill. Mark was big, bearded, young and impetuous. His brown eyes laughed at the world. Wherever he went there was noise and excitement, and boisterous singing. He dressed outrageously, today wearing blue cord breeches and a scarlet shirt, an emerald green cravat spilling out of his dark blue jacket. Hair and beard flourished together. His ready anger flare at those around him, or those he felt incompetent. He railed at morality. He liked Steven, who found pleasure in his company and was entertained by his vigorous personality, and whose cattle were models for his drawings, which were brilliant, vivid and instant images, beasts springing to exultant life from his pen.

Fenn nodded. He had never been out with the beagles before, although they often crossed his land. He knew both Master and Huntsman well, meeting them in the Grey Goose at night. The Master, Jack Dodds, was a farmer from the other side of Eagle Hill. He kept sheep, but as the Motorway was due to run through his land he no longer bred them. He bought in at the sales, fattened the lambs on rich grass and sold at a profit. It was stopgap farming at best and did not please him, but the profits were good and he did not intend to be caught with a pedigree herd that he valued when at last the pundits made up their minds and finally purchased his ground.

Meanwhile he bred beagles, and the pack was an all-consuming interest. He bred for speed and nose and valour and his hounds were known all over five counties. So was his Huntsman, a remarkable man who had retired, while still young, from a confectionary business that bored him, and had bought a small holding. He kept four cows, two pigs and five sheep and grew flowers which he sold to the local green-grocer. He spent hours studying birds, kept a peregrine fal-con which he flew at the sparrows that plagued his raspberry canes, and proved to have such an affinity with hounds that he could apparently think the pack into obedience most of the time.

His name was Ed Lucas, and he was a lean man; long-jawed, long-legged, with a tireless step, an infinite know-ledge of hares and a vast patience with hounds, although he had none at all with men, whose idiocies infuriated him.

Fenn watched, fascinated, as the pack was called to order, and the hounds set off, each flop-eared beast excited and eager. He admired the small stocky bodies, the gaily wav-ing sterns, the proud heads and the set of sloped shoulders and the neat cat-footed paws, well adapted for running over the rough ground that the hares frequented. Behind the pack the men followed, a few women among them, straggling down the lane.

Autumn had stripped the hedges of leaves but left bright berries and grey wiry tangles of old man's beard, and a few last late blackberries. The trees showed their outlines to the world, naked black, etched against a greying sky, next season's buds tucked tight on every twig, a promise of future abundance. A blackbird sang alone, his song throbbing through the air, his small body perched on the ultimate tip of a hawthorn tree.

The hills were blue mist, patched with brown. Steven Fenn was conscious of every aspect of the day, savouring it with the eyes of a newcomer. He would never tire of the lanes, the neatly latticed hedges, the flower and fern strewn banks, the pied patchwork of fields spread over the slopes, the chatter of water flowing into the brimming ditch from a pipe in the muddy bank, or the sudden flurry as an inquisitive horse galloped along the far side of the hedge and thrust a curious head over the stone wall that was built at the corner.

They stopped for a moment to gentle the animal, which was Mark Tilley's hunter, Tyrant – a quiet gelding that did not live up to his name.

The hounds turned towards a farmyard. One of the hands grinned, opening the gate. He had seen the hare in the field only half an hour before and knew that the scent would lie.

The beagles fanned over the ground, which was ripe for the plough once the weather improved, for this was the end of the wettest summer for more years than even Herbert Green, the landlord of the Grey Goose could remember, and that was a mighty long while. Water lay in the hollows, the becks and pools overflowed and marshy ground was so flooded that duck swam where, in other years, kingcups flourished and children came to pick them.

'Call him Rack . . . Racket would be a better name.' The Master suddenly exploded as the lead hound yelled at the top of his voice and changed course, the pack spilling behind him. 'He's too noisy by half.'

Mark, who knew the beagles well, and often acted as whipper-in, pointed them out by name to Steven Fenn, who was enjoying the rare break from the chores of his farm. He was playing hookey, and the nagging feeling of tiny guilt only served to enhance his pleasure.

'Rack . . . and Ruin behind him. Rack is too noisy and Ruin runs mute, which is just as bad. He's quick to pick up a trail and follow it, but as he doesn't call, he leaves the others behind. The odd looking white beast is Flotsam; his colour's queer, but he's a splendid nose, and he usually grabs the mask when they kill. That's not very often. Hares are a sight too clever.'

'Not this one,' Fenn said.

She had leaped from her form and stood for a minute, as if watching the pack. Then she turned and took off uphill, her ears and head bobbing above the bracken. She knew her way well and within seconds was running freely on the hard path that had been beaten flat by her frequent forays. The hounds gave tongue, and began to follow fast, Rack losing the lead to Flotsam, Ruin running ahead, nose down, silent, while Flotsam sang and the others joined him, and their chorus could be heard from every farm and cottage in the village.

The hare turned in her tracks and swung downhill, startling the followers, as she seemed to be running straight towards them. She leaped sideways, and Fenn whistled. She must have cleared over fifteen feet in a single jump. A tiny run, another leap, and she was pelting for the boundary, while the hounds checked where the scent broke, and within seconds she had vanished.

The men made for the gate. No farmer would give thanks if the beaglers forced a break. The whippers-in circled the gap, but Flotsam knew the rules and Ed Lucas, the Huntsman, sent the hounds on, into a field of sheep that fled bleating in a massy herd, panic-mad.

The hare cleared the ditch, burst through the far hedge, and crouched at the side of a cowfield. She knew a place where a hole bored right through the bank, and as the cows moved forwards, curious, she raced towards it, and was through, running in mad March circles, round and round in the centre of the field.

'Crazy!' said Steven Fenn.

'Not so crazy,' Mark answered. 'Watch.'

Wider and wider she circled, the spiral growing each time, until at last she had bounded right round the edge of the field. She returned to her hole as the pack spilled through the gate, and caught the scent, caught an abundance of scent, and began to run crazy, blundering into one another, till the Huntsman called them to order. Even then they were bewildered, for the scent crossed and re-crossed the field, and none of them could find the right line.

Steven grinned as the hare bounded towards them, paused a moment, looking at them as if daring them to cry out to the hounds, and then, as someone saw her and yelled, she increased her pace and sped up the hill and vanished.

An inquisitive fox, not long past his cub-days, put his nose out of the hedge. Rack gave instant tongue and speedy chase, flying on his trail, the pack pell mell behind him. The whippers-in tried to head the hounds, the Huntsman

13

called them to order, but excitement had captured them, and they raced on, heedless, while the lads who had been at the rear of the followers, bored by the proceedings, woke to life and chased after them, urging them on, yelling at them, until the beagles were rioting and there was no chance at all of bringing them back until they lost the trail, or killed.

The fox, regretting his curiosity, fled for sanctuary, his ears ringing with the hound cry behind him. He had never been hunted before, and his heart thudded, and his mouth was dry and the beasts that panted after him were more than life size, terror beasts, slavering for his blood as he slavered for that of the bounding hare. Through the sheep and over the beck, leaping the water, to race through bracken, breath panting, brush waving, and turn downhill and make for the farm below.

Behind the chicken house, on to the outhouse, up to the top of the kitchen roof, up to the pointed gable above the porch, from there to an outlying corner of the house, bounding like a cat, to crouch behind the warm and sulphurous chimney and look down in panting terror at the milling hounds, the shouting lads, and the laughing men, entertained by the fox-face in so unlikely a position.

The Master and whippers-in met and spoke sharply to the lads, who, about to answer back, saw the anger on the faces of those around them, shrugged, and, out-numbered, departed, hastened on their way by Mark Tilley's sudden ferocity. The Huntsman called the pack to order. Winded, sheepish, the hounds walked quietly back to the waiting vans.

Fenn watched them go, curiously. They were sturdy merry little beasts, nothing like the heavy fellhounds that he had followed at home.

'Coming to the Goose?' Mark asked.

Fenn nodded. It would complete his day, and Sarah had promised to help Joey with the milking. He thought of them affectionately. He had inherited them with his uncle's farm six years before and never regretted it for a minute. Didn't come like that nowadays, and Joey could outwork any other man in the village even though he was over sixty and a bit to too partial to the bottle, and Sarah must be nudging as many

14

years as he. They often told him to go out and enjoy himself. It was the first time he had gone for a whole day. Not that he couldn't, but the farm absorbed him, and he could not bear to leave it.

The Grey Goose was warm and welcoming. Logs blazed in the wide hearth. Hunting prints, of horses, hounds and fox, made gay splashes on the white distempered stone walls. The flagged floor was worn with centuries of use. Rumour told that Cromwell had eaten in the old parlour. Dickens was supposed to have rested in the room above.

A group of men played darts, one of them chalking the score. The others laughed and teased him.

'Come on, now, its not a treble you're wanting, its one, just one, come on Bill.'

Bill grinned and threw his treble and drank his mug dry and shouted for more beer all round and the drinks on him as he'd won the game.

'Not yet, you haven't,' said a small thin man with bright blue pebble eyes and yellow teeth and a ragged ginger moustache that looked like a hen's tail. He threw swiftly and neatly. A log slipped in the hearth, flames flying, making shadows that startled a kitten playing on the rug so that it fled under a chair and watched the room suspiciously from wide frightened eyes.

Fenn settled himself in one of the old chairs and stretched his legs to the blaze. His feet were wet from wading over marshy ground that held the water from one year's end to the next. He was a large man, filling his clothes, his shoulders broad, his neck thick, a grey beard spilling from a jutting chin. Thick bushy hair matched the beard, bristling, usually, from under a greenish-brown soft brimmed hat that seemed so much a part of him that when, as now, he discarded it, his friends found him faintly indecent, like a uniformed policeman without a helmet. He wore his usual garb of tweed jacket, breeches and highly polished brown boots.

It was good to sit, to feel the warmth from the fire and listen to the talk around him. Talk of cattle and sheep and crops. Talk of the weather. Today had been damp but it

15

had not rained, and that was a change. Talk of prices and pigs and sheep. Of wool and dips and the price of feed, of the woman that was living with old John Gee and him a bachelor this fifty years, and with no sign of any such caper before.

'Housekeeper, he calls her and we all know what that means,' said one of the men, grinning, and drained his mug, and walked out.

'It's been a good day,' the Master said. 'Apart from the lads at the end of it.'

Fenn waited for someone to say that boys would be boys but nobody did, and he resisted the temptation. The Master and the Huntsman went out to see to the pack, and he drank his pint and called for another, and watched the flicker on the wall, and the glint of horse brasses in the ingle nook and the kitten dancing with its shadow, playing with a pheasant's feather that someone had brought to tease it, and left behind.

He listened to the talk around him, savouring every moment. He had lived on a farm, until his father died. When his mother married again they had gone to live in a town. She had hated animals, and would not hear of him becoming a farmer so that he had trained as a research chemist and worked in a factory for more years than he cared to recall. By the time he was married, and had four children, there was little hope of changing. The risk was too great, and his commitments too heavy.

But his uncle owned a farm and here they came for holidays, trebly welcome after his aunt died. Steven's children spent much of their time there, and he himself became engrossed in the cattle. Gradually he had invested, in a small way, buying two bullocks for fattening, and then four and then four more, each time using his profits to pay for his next investment, afraid to tell his wife of his secret hobby. In time he also owned half the milking herd, and the only letter of the week worth reading was that telling him of the progress of his beasts.

The children grew up and went away, one to marry and live in America, one of the boys to become a doctor, the

16

second an engineer. His younger daughter lived in London, and then, when his wife died suddenly, Steven decided to make the final break. He had gone to live with his uncle, become enthralled by the farm, and, when the old man died, found himself the owner of one of the best herds in the county, with enough money behind him to indulge his passion.

He picked up the grey kitten and sat, savouring its fervent purr. Small creatures always entertained him, and he derived great pleasure from the orphans of the fields. The bottle-fed lambs that needed his help, the greedy calves, emptying the buckets as he watched, snuffling and snorting into the milk. Even the youngsters of both bitches and cats. It was a rich and satisfying world, where every creature breathed and grew and depended on man for its existence. Much more rewarding than the sterile life he had left behind, the world of papers and reports and business deals, of exchange and manufacture of goods that he never saw, and produce that he never handled. He had soon graduated from research to aministration. Now, he worked with his hands, and used his strength, and every penny in the bank came from his own unaided effort. It was a good life.

He looked around him at the other men in the Goose, still talking farm talk. The Master who had taken the beagles home and returned. Jack Dodds, with over eight hundred sheep, one of the biggest sheep farmers in the place; Ken Martin, with his famous herd of Jersey cows, matched for colour, so that each beast was honey gold with a darkening head and huge lustrous eyes, a princess among cattle. No one but Ken could tell them apart, but he knew each one, by name and by nature, by her milking yield and her calves. His wife Mollie laughed at him, but was as proud of the herd as he, and petted all the beasts when they came to the yard at milking time.

Rick Waller, with his Herefords; Mart Lewin, with the pig farm where he was helping one of the Universities with research on nutrition. His baconers were renowned, and he swore by his own particular diet. The college had heard of his beasts and come to see him and now he was playing

17

with the professors, he said, seeing which sort of diet made the fattest pigs, which produced good lean bacon, which made for flavour, which for quick growth. It was also profitable, as he had a small grant towards the work, which had, so far, produced several crops of impressive animals, all when they were sold more than repaying him for the time he had spent.

Small scale farmers and large scale farmers. It was a close-knit compact community, and, because he had stayed so often with his uncle, when he finally inherited Hollow End, he was no newcomer, but familiar to them all and accepted at once. He had helped out at haytime and harvest, helped round up sheep and talked farm talk by the hour, leaning on the five-barred gates, admiring the herds of cattle, or the healthy flocks, saving up the farm talk to last him through the long year until his next summer break.

Herbert Green, the landlord of the Goose, who was over seventy five, but would only admit to sixty, came to stir the fire and waggle a finger at the kitten.

'Enjoy your day?' he asked Fenn.

The farmer nodded.

'Sorry I never went out before, but there's not that much time on a farm,' he said. 'I'd like another couple of hands, but where do you get them these days? Joey and I work at a pretty fair stretch and even then the jobs never seem to finish. And Sarah does her whack too.'

'She's a great old girl, is Sarah,' the landlord said. He swept the hearth and raked the ashes, so that the last logs blazed and the new wood caught.

'Nothing like a wood fire.'

It was getting late. Joey would need help with bedding the two horses, and the little jenny donkey came in at night now that she was in foal. And the dogs had to be fed and the geese and ducks penned, and the chickens made safe. The fox often came prowling, and more than once Fenn had been tempted to take a gun and shoot him. He put the kitten down on the earth. It mewed at him, annoyed. It had been warm and comfortable. The tiny beast began to swarm up his trouser leg, trying to get back to warmth and safety. The

18

men grinned as he detached it and dumped it on Jack Dodds' knee. No need for Jack to hurry back. He'd finished with the sheep for the day and completed the chores on his own farm. It was an easier life when there were no cattle to milk.

Steven went out into the lane. It was almost dark and an owl was hunting the hedgerow. His bitch, Bess, was lying patiently outside the door, come to look for him.

'You old fool,' he said, and stroked her silky fur. She was a shaggy beast of unknown parentage, more like a retriever than any other dog, but with a hint of many ancestors in her. No breeder would look twice at her, but she was a wonderful guard dog, barking at every stranger, and at night she slept on the mat by Steven Fenn's bed, making up to him for the loneliness of his empty room. He still missed Jenny, though she would never have agreed to come and farm. Funny how life turned out.

Bess followed at heel, her day complete. She could not bear Steven out of her sight and had spent the day lying at the gate, nose on paws, until Sarah had sent her out, exasperated, and told her to go to the Goose. Bess went.

'That dog can practically tell the time,' she said to Joey as he fastened the hose to the tap. The cattle were safe in the fields, but the yard, as usual, was a fair old mess and no one at Hollow End was going to bed with a dirty yard, no matter how late in the day, not with Sarah there.

Steven Fenn heard the swish of water as he came up the lane. He went through the field gate and into the orchard. The donkey was a faint shadow under one of the far trees. He whistled, and she came towards him, and butted him amiably, knowing that his presence meant food and warmth and water. She followed him to the end stable, where clean straw waited for her, and she watched as he flooded the place with light, and brought her special rations and teased hay into the hay rack, and filled a bucket and held it for her to drink.

When at last the jobs were done, and Sarah and Joey locked up for the night in the small cottage beside the old stone farmhouse, Steven Fenn went, as always when it was fine, and sat on the felled tree at the edge of the orchard.

Moonlight was faint, a flicker and gleam, lighting the browsing cattle in the field, and bright enough to show a silver glint on the backs of sheep grazing Eagle Hill beyond. There was a warm smell from the stables where Micky and Grey stood, their breathing slow and re-assuring, their movements gentle, as they waited for sleep. Soon they would lie down and forget the world.

Steven loved this last hour of his day. On these nights he smoked his pipe, and often brooded happily on the morrow. Tonight he spent looking back. It had been a good day, a rare day to remember, better than most, but all days were good now. It was strange, he thought, that a man could live for years and be only half alive. He had, he supposed, loved his life with Jenny and his children. But there had always been something lacking. His work had been interesting, absorbing, and congenial, but underlying it there was always a nagging dissatisfaction. Perhaps it came from working for a company, never able to benefit from putting more into the job than it demanded, never able to add to a basic salary by extra effort, tied by regulations, by committees, by restrictions and delays. Affected by every change in government policy, by credit squeezes and economy drives, by the inability to export to markets that had once been available, because of some high level squabble. He had travelled the world and come back home, glad to be there, but always with a hidden need to get back to the farm, to use his hands, to work with beasts and with the things that seemed more important to him.

Now, he was also, in many ways, bound by restrictions. But he could build up his herd, could buy in as many store beasts as he could fatten, could increase his flock, could work to improve his ground. He had built new strong modern byres, installed a milking parlour, put up a lambing shed where he and Joey could shelter at night and watch over the ewes. His hens were housed in new buildings, well fenced against the foxes, safe from marauding rats. His pigs had clean comfortable sties. His barns were high and filled with hay that he had grown himself.

Even the animals were rewarding. People let you down.

Often unconsciously. A man hoped for too much perhaps, and was hurt when his children grew up and became critical and went away, and was puzzled by his wife, who was often irritating and lacked understanding.

Beasts, on the other hand, gave so much satisfaction. Perhaps because so little was expected from them and they were grateful for the smallest attentions. Feed a cat on cold meat and a little milk, and it purred its pleasure. Stand at the stable door twice a day to talk to the horses and pat them and they rewarded a man with disproportionate devotion. And a dog would follow his master through hell itself and his affection would never flag.

His hand strayed to Bess's head. She was lying at his feet, enjoying this late night ritual. Her warm tongue acknowledged him, licking his hand, and her tail beat against his shin. A small amused smile flickered on his lips.

Here he belonged, among men who tended animals, among men who were weatherwise and hard working, never knocking off when a hooter blared, but labouring until all the beasts were milked and fed and bedded down and safe for the night. Men who fed their animals before they fed themselves, who sat all night with a calving cow or foaling mare, men who, when they heard of a beast endangered, came at once to help. As they had the day that Mick jumped the hedge and fell in the pond. Half the village lent tools or aid on that day, and offered advice, and transport. He had been very much a newcomer than, in spite of his long attachment to the farm.

The church clock struck the half hour. Almost tomorrow. He yawned, and knocked out his pipe and Bess stood, knowing that it was time to go. A last look at the cattle field. Shala, queen of the herd, stepped towards the gate.

She was an affectionate beast, and always came to both Steven and Joey when they passed, knowing they would stop and speak to her and to rub her smooth neck, while she made small pleased noises of ecstasy and pushed her head hard against the men, asking for attention. She led the herd, but did not boss it, and her calves were the finest that they had. Steven had no bull. A bull made a lot of work, and he had so many cows that A.I. was speedier and more efficient, even with the failure rate, and he could utilize the best bull in the county and build a better herd. He patted the sleek head, and then went to check the stables and the chicken house, although he knew that they were secure.

A shadow paused at the corner of the byre. Eyes glinted in the dark and Bess barked. He grabbed her collar, not wanting her to argue with the fox. The shadow was gone. The fox did not like men, or their dogs, or their guns, and had been startled to find anyone awake on the darkened farm. An angry swearing from the old Tom in the barn showed that he had passed that way. Fenn went to scratch Tom cat's head, and glanced up at the stack where Black Cat had hidden her kittens. Two of them were out and about on unsteady legs, playing with a straw. Black Cat cuffed them, and they vanished.

'Bed, lass,' Steven said, and Bess bounded towards the kitchen door and waited for him to open it.

The kitchen was warm. The Aga had been stoked for the night, and his pan of milk was keeping hot on top of it. He had left it longer than usual and a thick skin had formed. He poured some into a glass, and gave some to the bitch, and then, yawning, bolted the door and took the mug upstairs.

There was a book by his bed, and he settled himself to read, but the printed words bored him, and he began to work out the probable lambing yield next year. Three hundred ewes, and many of them would produce twins. It would be a bumper spring. He finished the milk and turned off the light, and Bess settled on the rug beside him. Bob the Labrador was on guard outside, lying in the warmth of the hay scattered at the foot of the stack. The scattering had puzzled Steven and Joey until waking early one morning, Steven had seen a stag dragging at the bales. The old boy was welcome. He was very old, too, his antlers going back, his body scrawny. Poor old beast.

A bumper year. This year had been particularly good. The farm was double the size it had been when he took it over. He wanted to expand. There was ample scope. His uncle had owned so much land, not all of which had been put to good use. By judicious cropping and manuring he had improved the grazing and added some of the marginal land to the farm, enriching it until he could run sheep on it. His mind filled with the thought of spring lambs, he fell asleep, knowing that he was a fortunate and contented man, who had come, though late in life, to achieve his ultimate ambition.

CHAPTER TWO

JOEY was also contented. He whistled as he went to call the cows for milking. He was a small man, with a wrinkled merry face and eyes that held an incorrigible twinkle. He was down to earth and earthy, his talk of bulls and cows and sheep, of mating and of manure; foul mouthed, often enough, with the men, he had to mind his tongue when Sarah was about, as she would brook no bad language.

'Enough of that,' she'd say, and Joey would meeken his talk. He was a little afraid of his wife, who had a ruling streak and a bossy way with her and a need to manage men and beasts. Her kindness made up for her often abrupt manner. Sarah would take over in a village cottage when the mother had another child, or help the district nurse if anyone was ill and needed visiting, and shopping done for them. Her small stocky body and brown round face and bright shrewd grey eyes brought a feeling of comfort to anyone who needed help.

Joey loved his herd. He was proud of the sheep, but the cattle were his chief concern. His father had been cowman at Hollow End, and so had his grandfather. Where there were Fenns there were Hardens. It was as simple as that. Pity he and Sarah had never had any youngsters. Though these days they didn't seem to want to go on the land. They'd have left home. There wouldn't be Fenns at Hollow End when the boss died, and that was a pity. Nor Hardens either. He wondered what would happen to the herd, and then grinned at himself. Good for a good many more years, both of them. See plenty more cows born and make it an even better herd, one of the best in the country. He patted Shala.

Good breeding there, and what was more, he knew

most of it, remembered her mother, and her grandmother, and her great-grandmother too. And his Dad had remembered even further back than that and remembered that first bull, old Rajah they'd called him. A right brute, he'd been, and had gored one of the summer hands to death. Never been a bull at Hollow End since. Some of the villagers said that the lad that died still haunted the lane. And you could hear a bull bellowing in madness on a still night for miles around, but Joey had never heard it. Didn't believe such tales, either, but for all that he sometimes lay awake at night and listened, a little fearfully, to the farm noises, lest something uncanny be added to them. And, although he never confessed this to a living soul, not even to his wife, he always came home after dark by the orchard gate and avoided the bend in the lane where the bull had committed his savagery.

He watched the cows as they walked into the yard. Shala knew the way and waited patiently for him to fasten her into the milking stall. Her head turned towards him, watching him, until he patted her, and then he fastened the cups. It was an automatic procedure, which he had perfected to a fine art. Soon the parlour rang with the thumping beat of the machine, and milk filled the containers. Sometimes the cattle were stubborn, but today, with the sun just lifting over the brim of the hill and the dew hazing to mist on the grass, lying low over the fields, will-o'-the-wisp drifting, so that only the backs of the browsing sheep showed on the upper slopes, today everything was perfect. Joey whistled as he let the cows out into the rear yard, and led the next dozen in for the milking.

Sarah was boiling pigswill. Steven released the chickens into the runs and fed them. He did not like them running loose around the yard, but gave them plenty of room behind wire. If they were free the cats might get them, or they ran amok in the house making a fine old mess, or got into the fields and laid under the hedges. A rare old nuisance. He watched as they bickered over the grain and the usual flock of sparrows and starlings and pigeons joined them. Time for another shoot and maybe he'd get Ed Lucas to bring his peregrine and see if they couldn't get rid of a few. A right pest, both sparrows and pigeons, especially when it came to sowing crops. They'd take the seed and the new young shoots. And there were far too many of them.

When the cattle were back in the field Steven fed the dogs, a small token meal, as they had their food at night. He looked over the pigs. The twelve little ones in the far pen came squealing towards him and he noted with approval that they were already more solid and almost twice as big as two weeks before. They grew fast when they were very young. The sow grunted, finding parenthood a trial. Her brood stampeded past her, over her, and then settled to suck. She glanced up at Steven from small bright eyes. He rubbed her neck. He had not realized, until he came to keep them, that pigs were both intelligent and clean. Providing, of course, that they were decently kept. Too many backyard pigs had only half a chance. Needed good food and clean sties and proper bedding. Otherwise the piglets sickened and died.

'Bet's got an abscess just above her hoof. Cut it on something, I should think,' Joey said. Bet was one of the milking cows.

'See to her when I see to Black Cat. She's been fighting a rat.' Steven was used to coping with the beasts. Had to learn to do much of it yourself or vet bills were astronomical and in any case the vets couldn't cope. Any farmer worth his salt knew when to give a cow a drench or how to deal with an abscess or with the minor complications of calving, or with a case of scour.

Shala was waiting at the gate expectantly.

Joey laughed.

'Dunno what she'd do if I weren't here,' he said, diving into his pocket. He produced a huge hunk of bread. Steven watched with amusement, never failing to be delighted by the absurd sight of Joey holding the bread in his mouth while Shala delicately took it from him, and tossed it and caught it and ate it with satisfaction.

'Depraved, that's what you are,' Joey told her, and scratched her neck. She went on rubbing her head against the gatepost long after he had gone. At night, after milking, she was privileged and followed him to the cottage and put her head in at the window for her bread.

'You daft old fool,' Sarah always said, but on two nights when Joey had been ill she had held bread for the cow, although she would never have admitted it. She could not bear the sight of the beast's face when she found no one waiting for her, and Steven had not known, the first night, that Joey had gone home with a sore throat and been sent straight to bed.

The village children knew of Shala's habit, and sometimes came to watch.

'Have to charge and make a profit,' Joey had said one day, after putting on a demonstration for five small girls who had passed by on their way home from school.

'Looks like being a fine autumn for a change,' Steven Fenn said, as Joey passed him on his way to clean up the milking parlour.

'About time,' Joey answered. 'It's been a rare wet summer, and its not been dry underfoot for days. Had a lot more foot trouble than usual this year.'

Steve nodded. There had been several cases of foot rot among the sheep, but it seemed to be under control. The cattle were suffering too, and much more prone than usual to infected cuts and scratches on their legs. It couldn't be good for them to stand in mud all the time, and the pastures had suffered badly. The grass was trampled and mired, and in many places ruined, and would not recover until spring. He moved the cows from field to field, but even so it was hard to keep them on good ground. There would be need for hay this winter.

'The jenny's foal's due soon,' Joey commented, swilling water across the yard. 'In about seven weeks, I'd guess. Just after Christmas.'

'And Bess's pups.' Steven laughed. 'With Bob for father and Bess's mixed ancestry, I wonder how they'll look. They mated six days ago.'

'Right old mixture,' Joey said.

'Nice morning,' a voice called over the gate, and the men turned, to see Ed Lucas watching them.

27

'Wanted you to bring your peregrine and get a few of those damned pigeons out of my hair,' Steven said. 'Never seem to aim straight when I shoot them, and in any case, the peregrine's quicker and kinder than a gun.'

'I'll be over,' Ed promised. 'I came to say we're taking the beagles out again next week and wondered if we can come over your land?'

'As long as the gates are shut,' Steven answered. 'I'm knocking off for a cup of coffee. Join me?'

Ed Lucas came in, looking about him curiously. He rarely came to Hollow End, and Steven had made a lot of improvements. Seemed to be something new almost every time he passed. Must have sunk a pretty penny into the farm. Ed admired the alterations wholeheartedly. Envy had never been one of his faults.

The coffee was waiting. Sarah took Joey's out to him, and took her own cup into the sunshine, and sat for a moment, savouring the break from work. The sun was warm on her back, shadows spilled over the cobbles, and all around her were the noises of the farm. Bleats from the sheep on the hill, an occasional gentle lowing from the cowfields, the cluck of the chickens, the companionable grunting from the pig sties. There was always some noise, something happening, a busyness and bustle, even if it only came from the sudden scurry of the ardent cock, or the bark of a dog at a passing car.

Black Cat had caught a mouse, and was looking at it thoughtfully, wondering whether to deal with it herself or give her kittens a taste of blood. Sarah could almost see the cat thinking, and then Black Cat picked up the mouse and turned into the barn. Time to teach the kittens what life was all about. Her small purposeful body disappeared into the darkness.

'Cattle look good,' Ed observed, gazing out of the window. The field was next to the farmhouse, and at times the cows looked in, astounded by what they saw. There had been a fence, but it had fallen down and it amused Steven to see an enquiring head look in at the window, although Sarah grumbled at the smears on the glass.

'They're fine,' Steven said. 'Best lot of calves we've had for several years. We only lost three of them. Two before birth and one from scour. Poor little devil hadn't any resistance. One was annoying though. A dog got into the field and chivied poor old Bluebell and she panicked and rushed off and managed to push through a gap in the hedge and get out on to the road. She's scared stiff of cars, so when one got behind her she ran for miles, and the fool hadn't the sense to stop and turn her for home.'

'People don't know,' Ed said. 'Not unless they're farm reared. They do some damn silly things. Someone was feeding the hounds with toffees last week. Two of them got their jaws stuck up and you never saw such a mess. Took hours to clean them up. Messed up all the fur round their jaws and stuck in their teeth. Poor brutes went barmy.'

He stopped to drink and to munch one of Sarah's ginger cakes. She had a hoard of recipes that her mother had collected, and her cakes and biscuits were in high demand for local bazaars and coffee mornings.

'There's a sale of beasts over at Purway next week,' Ed said. 'You going over?'

Steven shook his head.

'Waiting for the big Beast Sale,' he said. 'I've got five heifers to put in. They aren't up to much. Disappointing animals, all of them. And I want to replace those and add another twelve, to make one hundred and eighty cows. I'd like to get the herd up to two hundred next year. After that I breed only my own. Got about seventy of my uncle's herd, but I wanted more beasts.'

'A lot of work,' Ed said.

'It's worth it.' Steven poured a second cup of coffee for each of them. 'I like working for myself. It's a rare treat after being part of a big company. You appreciate being your own boss, making your own decisions.'

'And banking your own profits,' Ed said, grinning. 'You've done a lot of work here. What are all those new buildings?'

There was nothing Steven liked better than to show off his farm, and Ed was an enthusiast, interested in everything, knowing enough to appreciate the latest developments. The new lambing shed, where the ewes were brought when birth was imminent, and Steven or Joey could spend the night in the warm, checking for difficulties. No more standing on icy ground, or bringing a sick lamb in from the hill and missing another awkward birth. No fear of marauding foxes, ready to snatch a newborn weakling. And Sarah was close, with bottles waiting in warm water, ready to help any small beast that needed her.

It was a light clean airy place, and the central heating, from radiators run off a gas boiler, ensured that there was no risk of fire. In one small section infra-red heat could be given to any ewe or lamb that needed it, and there was a camp bed on which the shepherd could rest between whiles, and hot water so that he could clean himself properly, and a small electric hotplate where a kettle could be boiled or a pan put to heat.

'Must have cost a pretty penny,' Ed said, and then regretted his outspokenness. He had not meant to comment. 'It'll be good to use it, though. Not been christened yet. Hope it repays you.'

'My uncle left a tidy bit. And I've saved all my life, and my wife inherited a big legacy and left it to me. When my father died he left all his money to my children, to save two lots of death duties. So I've no need to save a penny. Better to use it now than leave it to the government. They don't encourage a man to have faith in them or their ploys. Never did have any time for politicians anyway.' Steven closed the door behind him. They crossed the yard.

'Who does? Except politicians,' Ed said. 'This the milking parlour?'

Steven showed him the place. Everywhere was immaculate. Joey took as much pride in the farm as if it belonged to him. Beyond the parlour were the new winter quarters for the cows, complete with a conveyor belt system of automatic feeding, and with piped water leading to the troughs.

'I've got a heater in the tank to keep it from freezing,' Steven said, as he pointed to the massive metal container outside in the yard.

'Heard of a farm that had an immersion heater put in last year,' Ed said, leaning over the pigsty wall to scratch the old sow's back. She grunted blissfully. 'The workmen managed to earth the heater to the cattle trough. Farmer came in and found twelve dead cows.'

'Must have pleased him,' Steven said. 'I hope the contractors paid up.'

'He had to take them to court. They paid, but it don't make up for the loss of the cows, the calves, and the milk.'

'Nor the breeding,' Steven said. 'Part of my herd goes back to my grandfather's time ... There's other cattle from the same line of course, but we kept the best. And believe me, we've got some grand beasts. Shala's all set for a championship next year. She'll walk away with it. Sending her down to London. It will be nice to have a few rosettes here, on the old dresser. Haven't shown any of the beasts yet.'

Mick and Grey put inquiring noses over the paddock gate. Shala, seeing visitors, came for bread, sure that she was required to show off her party trick. Joey, from the other side of the yard, saw her, and grinned. He pulled a hunk out of his pocket. Ed watched with amusement as the cow took it gently from between his teeth.

'You old idiot,' Joey said affectionately and scratched her glossy head. She rubbed against his shoulder and then walked away.

'Funny how you get attached to some beasts,' Ed remarked. 'This peregrine of mine now, he's a charmer. Got some pretty ways, and is as gentle as any bird I've ever handled. But the last one was a brute. He and I never got on, and although I was sorry when he started having fits and died, somehow I wasn't half as sorry as I will be when I lose this fellow. He's a good bird, too. Quick to learn, easy to handle, and does what I want. Old Jacky used to sulk. Get up in a tree and refuse to budge. I've never been so exasperated by a creature in my life.'

'I had a dog like that,' Steven said. 'I like dogs, but this one tried my patience beyond measure. Hadn't a single endearing trait about him. He would run off, and then he took

31

to chasing sheep over at Lane Ends. Jock McClean rang me up to say he was sick of the brute, so I told him to shoot him next time he found him on his land. Can't say I was sorry. But if anyone ever lays a finger on my bitch Bess or old Bob, I think I'd pummel the living daylight out of him!'

Ed nodded. It was a point of view that he understood very well.

'Some people say that animals have human attributes,' he said, suddenly recalling a violent argument he had had one night in the Grey Goose, when one of the salesmen had said that his dog was almost human.

'They can say what they like. What they forget is that we're all animals,' Steven said. 'It's not so long since men crawled out of the muck and began to use their brains. For my money, they haven't used them to much advantage. We aren't much more than barbarians. We still have all the jungle passions ... fear and lust and jealousy and greed.'

'Humans!' Sarah said. She had been sweeping the yard and overheard their conversation. 'Beasts don't make war or drop bombs on each other, or burn women and children with napalm. Beasts don't lie and cheat and murder. They kill to eat, not for fun. Beasts, if you ask me, are a sight better than men. And they don't get stinking drunk either,' she added. Joey had been known to come crawling home in a pretty bad state on occasion, after a celebration. She stumped off into the farmhouse.

'Beasts don't bore you with their aches and pains either,' Ed said, laughing. 'Poor Sarah. Joey been up to no good again?'

'Not for a while. She gets upset by the news on the television. They showed some of the bombing of the villages in Vietnam last night. For all her tough appearance Sarah's soft centred. See her with a baby animal, and you'd not know her. Though she'd never admit it. She sounds acid enough, but that that's all camouflage.'

'Sarah's always there at a birth or a death ... helping out, and never a word of complaint at being called out at night if someone's in trouble. You're lucky to have the pair of

32

them. And anyone would think the farm was theirs the way they talk. Proud as if they owned the beasts.' Ed was walking towards the gate at the other side of the cobbled yard.

'They do own some of the bullocks,' Steven said. 'Sarah came to me last year and asked if she could invest some of their savings in five bullocks. She reckoned she'd earned the grazing, and she'd been told by a farmer lower down in the village that we don't carry as many bullocks on the land as we can. So Joey came with me to the Beast Sale and picked his beasts and sold them for a tidy profit. This year ten of our thirty bullocks belong to him and Sarah. We've put another field under grass and next year they want to add even more beasts of their own. It's a very good idea . . . adds to their income and stimulates their interest. And they deserve it.'

'See you tonight in the Grey Goose?' Ed asked.

Steven nodded.

'It's good to get out for an hour or so and have a change of company. Those arguments down at the Goose keep me on my toes,' he answered.

Ed grinned.

The Goose had more arguments to the hour than there were glasses on the shelves. The men argued about everything . . . the way to fatten cattle, the methods of rearing stock, whether battery hens were better than those running free, about de-beaking hens and de-tailing cattle, about barley beef and about the best winter feed, and the best fertilizer. It was a free-for-all in which everybody joined, and the fiercest of all the arguments started when they began to discuss the government, and the way in which a farmer was regimented, by forms and facts and figures, and the new ideas that few of them liked and none of them agreed with.

Steven whistled to Bess and went to look over the sheep. He enjoyed the stimulus of outside company. He enjoyed every minute of his long day. He enjoyed his beasts and his farmhouse and he enjoyed planning and scheming and seeing new calves jump in the meadows. He was longing for spring and for the new lambs. Life was very good.

A magpie flew up from the long grass in the meadow, and

33

suddenly, superstitiously, he crossed his fingers, remembering Jenny had always said that the birds were unlucky. But what was there that could go wrong now? Other than the usual crop of winter ills.

A second magpie joined the first. Jenny used to say 'One for sorrow, two for joy.'

That was better. Even so, a tiny nagging unease be-devilled him. Life was too good, and some age-old atavistic instinct told him to beware. Good fortune could not last. And surely his was too good to be true?

He shrugged and grinned ruefully. He was getting softening of the brain. He began to round up the sheep, and forgot his uneasiness.

CHAPTER THREE

THE Grey Goose was crowded. It was the Master's birthday, and half the beagle followers were there to toast him. The landlord was extra busy, but did not care. He liked to see the place full, the men happy, the glasses brimming. He piled logs on the fire, rubbed the cat's soft back with his slipper-shod foot, and listened to the till ringing cheerily. It was the best night they'd had for weeks.

Ed Lucas sat in the corner, his peregrine on his gloved fist. The bird was used to people, used to being taken in Ed's car, used to handling and attention, and it watched the room with bright eyes, its head turning from side to side. The cat was wary but unbothered. Ed often brought a bird with him when he came for a drink. He had kept all sorts in his time. A jackdaw, an owl, and a sparrow hawk within Steven Fenn's memory.

Bess had come down with Steven tonight and tucked herself under the table, head on his foot. There were also two sheepdogs and a cross bred lurcher, all keeping one eye open, but all sleepy and warm and disinclined to argue with one another. Their masters drank and laughed, and in the corner Mark Tilley was singing a folk song. Soon he would dominate the room, but just now he was more interested in watching and sketching the quick interchange of expression on the faces around him, and his song was almost involuntary. He always sang when he sketched. Steven sometimes thought Mark must have been born with a pencil in his hand. All his thoughts expressed themselves through his clever fingers.

Steven sat quietly, watching. He was, as always at the end of the day, extremely tired. It was a long exhausting day, and it took time to clear up after the last milking, to bed down the horses, and brush them before nightfall, to call in the jenny donkey, who was still skittish enough to be reluctant to come to her stall, to lock up and make everything safe for the night. Joey and he were always glad to sit silent for the first half hour, relaxing sore muscles and easing their minds of the day's memories.

The Vicar was there, talking to the Master. They were old friends, and often challenged one another to a game of chess. Just now their talk was idle; of the weather, and the beagle pup that the Vicar's housekeeper was walking for the hunt, and the fund for the Church roof, a fund of which the Master was the Treasurer.

The night had turned stormy. Rain pelted on the windows, and wind lashed the timbered walls. The door was flung open and slammed shut, and two men came in, shaking raindrops from their hair and rain from their coats, and grinning at the men in the Goose, all of whom they knew well.

'Damned awful weather you have in these parts,' one of them grumbled. He was the younger of the two, a slight man of about thirty, his face lean, his hair dark and smooth except for one high wave above his right eye. He moved like an athlete, a complete contrast to his small, plump, elderly companion, whose thin grey hair was plastered flat to his head, and who looked round the room out of unhappy blue eyes that were thickly fringed with fair lashes.

'Double whisky,' he said. 'Bloody awful weather.'

He took his glass and walked over to the fire. The cat stretched, and seeing him, went into sudden ecstasy, rolling on her back, purring, every breath a rich throb. Her paws embraced his wet ankles and she rubbed her head ardently against his leg. His mouth relaxed into a small smile, and he stooped and picked her up and sat in one of the battered leather chairs, holding her against him.

'Damned if I know how you do that, Robbie,' the landlord said.

'Always did have a way with cats. I like cats. It's people I don't like,' he answered. Robbie Preston had been a reporter for more years than he could remember. His colleague, MacLinton, had worked with him for the last three years. He put his camera on the table. Both worked for the local paper.

'Same again,' Robbie said.

The landlord looked at him, sure that this was not the first double whisky or even the second of the day. But Robbie Preston could hold his drink.

'Not driving, are you?' he asked, bringing the glass over to the man.

'I'm driving, and I'll stick to bitter lemon tonight,' Mac answered. It was going to be a tough assignment getting Robbie home. They'd had one hell of a day. He grimaced. There were times when even he hated his job.

Robbie drank his third double whisky, and called for a fourth. He had only started counting at the Grey Goose. It was more convenient to forget the couple of drinks he had had at the Star, and the flask that had been full that morning and now lay empty in the glove compartment of the car.

'Hell of a day,' he said to the cat. The cat purred. 'Hell of a place. Hell of a job.'

'Bad job?' the Master asked. They all knew Robbie Preston.

'Bad?' Robbie frowned, and the cat eased itself more comfortably on his knees and began to lick his hand. The warm tongue pleased him, the purring cat relaxed him, and he began to release the day's pent feelings in a spate of talk.

'You know what I am?' He turned to look at the Vicar. 'I'm a ghoul. A ghoul. A vampire, fattening on my victims. Death. Blood. Murder. Disaster. Old Robbie'll go. Robbie'll tear your heartstrings, pull out all the stops, Robbie'll turn your guts to water, make you see the misery in our little stupid human world.'

He paused thoughtfully.

'It's not as bad as all that, surely,' Ed Lucas said.

'Bad? It's worse. It's hell, bloody damnation, purgatory. It's seeing people under strain and stress and people living through tragedy. Great occasions: men who climb mountains, men who sail round the Horn, men who travel to the stars, they aren't for Robbie. Robbie's the lad for the back-street brawl and the man who choked his wife, and the razor slash in the dark alley. Robbie's the man to talk to the widow and hear the kids yelling for a Dad who won't come home, he's dead, down in the mine. He's buried, in the ground, he's smashed up in his pretty new car, he's drowned deep in the sea. Or the girl who went out for a bright night and ended up raped and mangled. Go and see her mother, Robbie. You know how to handle them, old boy. God! They make me vomit.'

He looked up at faces that were pleasantly blurred, and once more focused on the Vicar.

'You wouldn't know. Nice safe job. Nice safe people. Thoughtful, kind, going to the Church bazaar. Singing hymns on Sunday. You don't get the other sort here.'

'We get them, Robbie,' the Vicar said. 'We get them all. Thieves and knaves and liars. Men who rape and men who kill. And I was at Cowthorne before you this morning. I stayed there too.'

'What happened at Cowthorne?' the Master asked.

'Read all about it. Read all about it in the Daily Nightmare. Harrow your guts on it, gloat on it, revel in it. Robbie Preston tells all. God Almighty, give me another drink. I'll tell you what happened at Crowthorne. I'll tell you all.'

'You've had enough,' Mac said.

'I've never had enough. Never enough to chase away the faces that look at me, the people that reproach me, the people I lay bare to the public view. Making news for ghouls and grave robbers, for vampires and harridans. There are still folk who'll knit round the guillotine, Vicar, and men who'll run a mile to see a nice bloody road accident, and women who'd hold their children in the air to see a public hanging. Only we don't do that any more. We don't hang men in public or guillotine them. We only flay them alive, tearing out their souls and putting them on paper for all the nasty morbid beastly minded world to gloat over.'

There was no stopping him now. The whisky was singing inside him, inspiring him to talk as he had never talked before and never would again. He could see the face of the old woman at Cowthorne's, see the mess, and see behind the face to the horror that would never die out of her mind.

'There were two old people at Cowthorne's,' he said. He held the cat against his face, deriving comfort. 'Yesterday they had money hidden under a floorboard in the kitchen, they had a nice home, and they had each other. Today the old man lies down in the morgue, battered and kicked to death by two young thugs who knew he had savings. They broke the furniture and slashed the bedding. They put a cord round the cat's throat and choked it. And they tied the old woman to the bed and hung her dead cat above her. Very funny they were. She lay awake till the milkman came, luckily at six thirty. She called him, and he found her. And the old man. And the dead cat. And the empty hole in the floor where they found his savings. And all she can say is that she hasn't a penny left in the world and she doesn't know what she's going to do. Only consolation is the police dog found the thugs – but no punishment can make up for what they've done.'

He held out his glass. Mac nodded to the landlord. Robbie couldn't take it, never had been able to take it. He should have changed his job. Poor old Robbie. Trouble was although he said he hated people, he really loved them, he understood them, and he felt their sorrows as much as he did his own. There wasn't room in the world for indignation and sorrow for others. A man had to insulate himself. Pretend it didn't matter, laugh at what went on in the world outside. There was too much to worry about, and it didn't do any good. If he stopped to think about it he'd have to drink as much as Robbie. He turned his head and saw the Vicar watching him and wondered uneasily if the other man had read his thoughts.

'You see. If disaster comes to Salem Hardacre, Robbie's going to be there. Good old Robbie.' He lurched to his feet, and put the cat down on the chair, and vanished unsteadily through the back door.

'Will he be all right?' Steven Fenn asked.

'He'll manage,' Mac said. 'He always does this after a bad case. He ought to find another job.'

'What job?' the Vicar asked drily. 'Robbie's been a reporter for over thirty years. Too old to change.'

'I did,' Steven said suddenly. It had not occurred to him before that he had in fact changed his job, and then at an age at which most men retired.

'You were never really anything but a farmer, all your life, Steven,' the Vicar said. 'Robbie's a born reporter. The pity is that he's so good at reporting disaster.'

'Death and disaster,' Robbie said, swaying in the doorway. His buttons were half undone, his tie under one ear, his face wet with sweat. 'Death and disaster. I hope they punish those little thugs. I hope they tear them limb from limb. I hope they rot in hell for ever. Will they rot in hell, Vicar? You believe in hell, don't you, and in Judgment? Well, I don't. I wish I did, but I don't. Judgment is mine, saith the Lord. It'd be nice to have a nice Lord sitting up there, ready to deal out to us what we all deserve ... dear God, I'm glad there's not. What would you say I deserve, Vicar? Robbie the ghoul, what does a ghoul deserve from his de-de-i-deity?'

'Come on, Robbie,' Mac said. 'Pay up and come home.'

'Home.' Robbie contemplated it with disfavour. 'That cold old place and that mean-faced old witch of a landlady. All the lights are to be out at ten, Mr. Preston. I can't have you bringing women into my house, Mr. Preston. Silly old cow, can't she see no woman would look at Robbie, poor old Robbie, what a mess! What a mess. I'm not paying, landlord, no money, put it on the bill ... charge it to the paper, charge it to the Vicar. Poor old Robbie. No money. She hadn't any money, They took it all. Put it on the slate, landlord. Come, landlord, fill the flowing bowl, and let it fill the Vicar.'

He began to laugh, and tears followed the laughter and streamed down his face. The Master took his arm and led him outside.

'I'll pay,' Mac said. 'He gave every penny he had on him to the old lady.'

He walked out. They heard Robbie retching outside in the gutter, and the Master came back, his face granite hard.

'Poor devil,' he said.

The landlord was looking at the money Mac had given him to pay for Robbie's drinks.

'He gave every penny he had on him to the old lady at Cowthorne,' he said. He set the money aside. 'I reckon she'll need more than that. It's time, gentlemen please.'

There were three pound notes on the counter. The men brought their glasses, and filed out, each man putting his hand in his pocket. When they had gone the landlord looked at the pile of notes, which had grown in size. The Vicar stood on the other side of the bar with Steven Fenn beside him.

'Nearly twenty-five pounds,' the landlord said.

'I'll take it to her when I go to the hospital.' The Vicar folded the notes and put them safely in his wallet.

'People aren't so bad, after all,' he said.

'Some of them.' The landlord was terse.

It had been an eventful evening. He turned on the wireless for the news.

'Four cases of foot and mouth disease have been reported in farms on the Shropshire border,' a dispassionate voice said. 'All the beasts on all four farms have been slaughtered to prevent the outbreak spreading. Farmers are asked to examine their beasts carefully.' The landlord switched the set off.

'I never thought of that.' Steven's mind was suddenly full of the farm and the numbers of animals on it. Cattle, sheep, pigs. All potential victims, if the epidemic spread.

'It's a long way from here,' the Vicar said consolingly. 'Coming my way, Steven?'

Steven nodded, and tried to keep his mind on the conversation as they walked down the lane. But the news had unsettled him. Only yesterday he had been unable to think of any disaster that could strike his farm and change his good

41

fortune. Now, one tiny invisible microscopic bug could leap out of the air and wreck all his work and his hopes. It was a long way away. Even so, he lay awake worrying long after he had gone to bed.

CHAPTER FOUR

It was a fine week-end, a fact that Steven Fenn viewed with considerable misgiving. Fine weather brought the people out from the towns, brought the cars and bicycles, brought the picnickers, and the ramblers. Fine weather meant broken walls and fences, litter in the fields and along the lanes, cars parked in farm gateways, blocking his own vehicles, children trampling in the meadows, bruising the hay, and dogs romping in the sheep fields.

'Going to be a hot day too,' Sarah said, as she took the cattle back to the field and closed the gate on them. It was the end of October and remarkably warm and sunny. Shala butted her head against Steven's broad shoulder, asking for attention. He scratched her head between the ears and she sighed blissfully, dreamily content. She had just been milked and the sun was warm on her back and she was supremely comfortable.

'Never thought I'd hate to see the sun,' Steven said. 'People get worse every year. Make more and more mess.'

'Just because there's more and more of them,' Sarah said. 'And Salem Hardacre's always been a show village. Not many villages left with the green in front of the church and the old almshouses, and the timbered manor with its lakes and park.'

By lunchtime there were five cars parked in the lane. Steven did not mind so long as they kept away from his fields, but just as he was sitting down to his own meal of cold meat and pickled beetroot he heard a commotion in the yard.

Joey came into the room, his face set, and picked up the shotgun and loaded it.

43

'Damned dog in the sheep field,' he said, and raced out, whistling to one of the sheep dogs that was lying comfortably in the shade by the haystack. The dog came running, delighted to be noticed. Steven hurried after them, swallowing hastily.

The sheep were milling dementedly, a romping spaniel barking at their heels. Steven swore, and called Bob, and then yelled at Joey who was brandishing the gun furiously. He had sent the sheepdog to herd the sheep away from the chasing dog.

A distracted man and woman stood beside the gate of the sheep field. The man was calling.

'Here, Bobsy, here, good dog, heel, Bobsy.'

'Don't shoot him. He doesn't understand,' the woman cried out, as Joey plunged into the field.

'Joey!'

Steven's bellow stopped the little man in the act of raising the gun to aim.

'We'll teach the dog a lesson, not kill it,' he said grimly. He turned to the dog's owners.

'Since you can't stop your dog chasing my sheep I will. You're lucky that I don't have my man shoot it. Now, if you can, call him off, and quick. Otherwise he's going to have a nasty shock.'

'Bobsy!'

It was useless. The spaniel had never had such fun before in all his pampered life. He snapped excitedly at one of the biggest ewes, and she plunged headlong towards the corner of the field, thrust her body through the hedge and landed on her back in the trough of water on the other side. Joey swore and put aside the gun and ran to pull her out, and the woman blushed, not having heard such language before. Joey was not mealy spoken at the best of times.

'Get him, Bob,' Steven said, looking down at his Labrador, who had waited quietly at heel. Hours of training had turned Bob into a most obedient dog, and Steven was proud of him. He was a powerful beast, one of the largest of his breed that anyone had seen. The spaniel's owners watched white-faced as he ran across the field, and intercepted the spaniel by catching him by the throat.

The spaniel snarled and attempted to twist out of reach, the sheep forgotten. He did not like the look of the dog that had attacked him, but he was no coward and within seconds the two animals were snapping and biting, each trying for a better grip on the other.

'Stop them, please stop them,' the woman said. 'My poor Bobsy.'

Steven glowered at her. Bob could look after himself and he did not care if the other dog was mangled and had to be put down, but he went over and grabbed the Labrador by the scruff, and pushed the spaniel clear with his booted foot. It ran, tail down, whimpering, back to its owners, who lifted it and comforted it.

'You brute,' the woman said venomously.

Steven looked at her contemptuously, his mouth grim.

Joey came over towards them carrying one of the smaller ewes. Blood poured from her throat.

'Have to put her down,' he said. He put the ewe on the ground.

'That's just one sample. God knows what else your damned idiot dog has done.'

'It wasn't Bobsy,' the woman said. 'He's a gentle dog.'

Steven bent over the spaniel and forced its mouth open. Wool was caught between the animal's teeth, and there was blood on the wool. The man put his hand inside his jacket and drew out his wallet.

'How much?' he asked.

'Get out,' Steven said furiously. He took the gun, which Joey had leaned against the hedge. 'Just get out. And if I see that dog among my sheep again, I'll shoot him immediately.'

He watched them walk away, the dog still whimpering.

'What a dreadful man!' the woman said, before they were out of hearing. 'My poor poor battered Bobsy.' She kissed the dog's head.

Steven looked at Joey.

'My God!' he said.

He bent to examine the ewe.

'Will she be all right?'

Joey nodded.

'It's not half as bad as it looks. I stopped the bleeding, and just let the blood flow again to scare the fools. A couple of stitches and she'll be fine. That dog won't chase sheep again. Put the wind up them proper.'

'Pity Bob didn't do a bit more damage. They might have spread the word,' Steven said. He patted the Labrador. 'Good dog, then. Let's have a look at your war wounds.'

Bob had a nicked ear and a bite on his shoulder, but was otherwise unharmed. He was used to being damaged. No dog in the village ever trespassed on Bob's territory, which included the lane outside the farm as well as all the fields that his master owned.

Steven went back to his interrupted lunch of cold meat and pickles. Sarah cooked at night, a late meal when all the jobs were done, that they could enjoy at their leisure.

'More picnickers than ever,' she said, as she came in to clear the dishes away and wash up for him. 'Just asked a family to move from the field by the duckpond. Drove their car in and all. I don't know. Wonder what they'd do if I set up shop in their back gardens? Seem to think farmland's a sort of public park. I suppose it's because in a town every green space is public and they think the country's just one big park for their amusement. Never dream of asking please can they come on to your land.'

She shook her head over the oddities of townsfolk. The week-end would soon be over and life return to normal. It had taken Joey fifty minutes instead of the usual fifteen to drive to the other side of the village and pick up a piece of machinery that the blacksmith had mended.

By tea time on Sunday most of the visitors had gone, though their trail was left behind them, an idiot wake of paper and cardboard, of ice cream wrappers and bus tickets, of tins and bottles and newspapers. Joey's last job on a Sunday evening was to tour the fields and remove cans and bottles that had been flung over the hedges. It was too easy for a beast to cut itself on the jagged edge of an open tin or

46

to tread on a bottle and smash it, and then cut itself on the glass. Only the year before one cow had been lamed by a broken bottle that had fallen in a thick clump of grass and remained unseen, and Black Cat had hurt her head badly trying to get at fragments of salmon left in a half-opened tin.

Joey toured the field bordering the lane. He carried a sack with him, and it was more than half full before he had finished. He stood for a moment, watching the sun set behind the hill. The clouds were streaked with light, flushed with splendour, and the trees were brilliant with colour. It was a good time of day, and Joey, although he could never have said so, was passionately attached to everything that the countryside had to offer. His eyes revelled in the changing sky. He knew which clouds presaged wind and which threatened storm, or snow, or rain. He could, if he had words to use, describe every change in the seasons, the bleak black winter trees and drab dank fields, the fresh young green in the spring and the yellow of flowers in wood and field and hedgerow, the summer bright trees, changing to summer-sad-and-dusty before autumn blazoned every leaf and berry.

He put the sack down, and watched the day fade into night. The sheep were quiet, having circled the field. They began to feed in the far corner in the early dawn, by midday were opposite the farm, and by nightfall had worked their way to the sheltering trees, where they fed and drowsed, unless startled by a prowling fox into noisy flight. Their panic brought Bob at once from his corner in the yard. There was no danger when he was near. He chased off badger and fox and stoat and weasel, and protected every creature that was in his care.

The cattle were shadowy under the trees. Joey tried to pick them out, knowing from the markings on face and body and rump which beast was which. Shala, the prettiest of them all and the gentlest, was his particular favourite. Gentle to handle, easy to milk, co-operative at calving, and so proud of her latest offspring that she needed to show it to all of them, to Joey and Sarah and Steven, well aware of their praise. They were fine calves, Shala's calves, four little beauties she'd had over the years, all heifers, all now added to the herd. He had Meg in the calf pen, and Nandy in the heifer field, and Pet was in calf herself now, and Rena was somewhere in the shadows beyond the elm tree.

He picked up the sack. The bullock field was safely away from the lane, and there was no danger of rubbish lying there, but last thing at night Joey went to look at his own cattle, at the ten fine animals that were destined for the spring sales. They were wonderful beasts, putting on weight a treat. Every penny profit would be his . . . his and Sarah's. Sarah looked after their money, always had. Steven Fenn paid her her own wages and Joey's and Joey was given a couple of pounds for pocket money, for beer and for tobacco, and Sarah took the rest and banked it. She was a good wife, Sarah, for all her shrewish tongue and her lack of sympathy when he'd had one or two too many down at the Goose. Women never did understand that sort of thing – how one drink led to another when you were with your mates.

Joe shouldered the sack. He could see Steven Fenn sitting on the tree stump, Bess beside him, and Bob was standing in the corner of the yard, watching Black Cat show her kittens what to do with a mouse. The tiny creature ran every which-way, and the kittens pounced and patted and played, until Black Cat killed it with a sharp paw and quick bite, and the kittens fought each other and worried the tiny bleeding carcase. Didn't do to be sentimental about animals. Else the rats and mice would eat every grain in the place, and take over the house. Take over the world for that matter if you didn't keep them down. Some folk had funny ideas.

There was an odd noise in the cattle field. Bob barked, Bess stood up and stared into the darkness, Steven peered into the shadows and Joey ran. It was a noise he had heard before, and had hoped he would never hear again. One of the cows was choking.

The sound increased in volume, as if the beast was dying. The nearby cattle began to low uneasily. Sarah, always alert, came outside in her dressing gown, carrying the big lamp. Steven grabbed it and ran to join Joey. It was not easy to see in the darkened field.

Joey found the cow. It was Rena, Shala's daughter, one of their best milkers. A piece of polythene protruded from her jaws. She was trying to suck air in noisy uneven rasping gasps, almost totally unable to get her breath.

Steven knelt beside her with the lamp. Rena turned her head, knowing he would help her. Her agonized eyes looked up at the men, and the croak of her breathing distressed both of them. Joey was swearing under his breath, his hand in the beast's jaws, trying to extract the polythene from her gullet.

'God Almighty! There's yards of the bloody stuff. She's got most of it tangled in her guts.'

'I'll get the Vet,' Sarah said.

'Not going to do any good. She'll be dead before he comes.' Joey lapsed into obscenity, and Steven tried to move more of the polythene, but it was useless. The tormented breathing had stopped. The cow was dead. The Vet, arriving at top speed, found the pair of them trying to revive her with artificial respiration, having pulled the larger part of a long thick strip of polythene out of her mouth.

'It's useless, Steven,' the Vet said. 'It's right inside her. You've only pulled the end out.' He pushed his hand into her throat. There was yards of the stuff, long ribbons of polythene.

'Ed Lucas had the same thing happen to one of his sheep. People chuck anything and everything over the hedges. Fields are just waste ground to them. Don't stop to think of the poor wretched beasts. I've just stitched up one of the beagles. Cut its leg to the bone on broken glass that some fool had chucked in the brook down by the kennels. No end to the trouble summer visitors cause in this village. Better get the knacker out to that cow, Steven. I'm sorry. Nothing I could do.'

'I know that,' Steven said. 'Rena was one of our best cows. And we had a sheep savaged by a dog yesterday. Be glad when winter comes and the damned tourists leave us in peace.'

'Savaged by a dog called Bobsy,' the Vet said. 'Bob knows where to bite, doesn't he? I put eleven stiches in the brute, and heard all about your wickedness.'

'I was blazing mad,' Steven said.

'Don't worry. I read them the riot act and Bobsy didn't get any sympathy from me. As soon as I heard that a farmer had set a vicious Labrador on to their dog I knew that it had been worrying your sheep. Know you too well to think you'd put Bob on to another dog for fun.'

'By the way,' he added, as he turned to go, 'there are another five cases of foot and mouth disease reported today. They're a goodish way from here, but you know how it spreads. Keep an eye on your beasts and let me know at once if you see anything unusual, and I'll contact the vets dealing with the outbreak. I'm going to warn the other farmers here tomorrow. Can't be too careful. Not when it means slaughtering all your beasts if one gets it.'

'And a bloody silly policy that is,' Joey said. 'Like killing off a whole family because one of them gets flu.'

'It's not like flu at all,' the Vet said. 'More like cholera or smallpox. Anyway, forewarned is forearmed, and I don't suppose that it will reach epidemic proportions. We haven't had a bad outbreak for over ten years.'

'Have to get the tractor and move that poor brute into the yard,' Joey said. 'Foot and mouth. That's all we need. Used to cure it with tar and drenches in the old days. I remember in 1922 . . .'

'Let's get to bed,' Steven said. The day had gone on long enough. He had no desire to contemplate the loss of any more beasts. He would collect the insurance on Rena, but it didn't make up for the loss of her milk, and she would, in time, have succeeded Shala as queen of the herd.

Damn all summer tourists. Why couldn't they educate people properly? His family had been country trained when the kids were very small, Jenny had seen to that.

He helped Joey tie the cow to the tractor and watched him bump away. It was an undignified end. He'd have to call the knacker in the morning. He walked across to the stable to look at the little ewe. She seemed to have come to no harm

50

and that at least was one good thing. He whistled Bess. Bob went to lie in the straw by the haystack, and Steven went wearily to bed, his mind full of facts and figures. Tomorrow he must look up the veterinary dictionary and see if there were any precautions he could take to keep his beasts free from foot and mouth. Three hundred sheep and one hundred and eighty cows and dear only knew how many pigs. And the heifers. And the bullocks – couldn't sell anything now. Sarah said the big sow had farrowed that morning, and he hadn't counted the piglets. The fear that had troubled him vaguely the night before returned in force, so that he lay and listened to the church clock striking the quarters, to the sound of cattle lowing in the distance, and to the keening owl brooding in the elm tree, hungering for mice.

He thought of the magpies and of Jenny's superstitious fear of them, and he wished that Jenny was lying beside him, her breathing livening the deserted room. He put down a hand and Bess licked it and turned into a more comfortable position and went to sleep. The clock struck again. Only three hours to cockcrow. Steven went downstairs and made himself a milk drink. The Aga was low, and he banked it up, and looked out of the back door and spoke to Bob, who came to him eagerly, overjoyed to find anyone awake at such an hour. Dawn was more than a rumour in the mist before Steven finally went to sleep.

CHAPTER FIVE

Two nights later Steven called in at the Grey Goose. There were few people there. The Vet had dropped in to look at the cat, who had developed an abscess on her neck, having argued with the old grey Persian three doors away. She lay on the hearth looking sorry for herself, with the hair shaved away from the bite, and a slightly uneasy expression on her face as she watched the man fill his hypodermic syringe.

'Nobody here tonight,' Steven said, taking a pint mug to the chair nearest the fire. He knelt down and held the cat, who was preparing to run. She hated injections and squalled loudly as the needle sank deep. Bess gave her an interested and inquisitive glance, saw the syringe, and hastily crouched and eased herself out of sight under the settee. The men laughed.

'Been meaning to get rid of that battered old thing,' the landlord said, 'but obviously it has its uses!'

'There's more foot and mouth on the other side of the county,' one of the men said. 'Going to declare an infected zone. We'll be just outside it, but the Beast sale's off. And no more beagling.'

'That means I've got to keep my five heifers for a bit,' Steven said. 'I wanted to get rid of them. They're none of them much use, I don't know why. Came from some of my best milkers, too.'

'Probably the bull,' the Vet said. 'I suppose you used A.I.?'

Steven nodded.

'We don't want a bull. Too much trouble. Makes extra work and they're tricky beasts. Though sometimes I feel I'd like to rear one of my bull calves. Had some little beauties. If Shala ever has a bull calf I might be tempted.'

'Village won't forget the bull that used to be at Hollow End.' The landlord of the Grey Goose could remember all that had happened in Salem Hardacre, remember back to the years before the Great War when there had been horses and carts instead of cars, and no tractors, and the big shire horses to pull the ploughs.

He could remember the village when they held ploughing matches on the far field at Hollow End, and remember days when the Goose had been filled with men celebrating one victory or another. Nothing was the same now. They had been good days, and these were bad days. Money had been tight but there hadn't been the rules and regulations, and men could laugh at a joke. Now everyone looked grim and everyone was in a hurry and the days seemed shorter and the world seemed smaller, and much more misery in it. Only had to look at a paper, and see the pictures of disasters everywhere. Fire and flood, famine and earthquake, war and devastation.

'What can we do about foot and mouth?' Steven asked, as the Vet put away his hypodermic, and stroked the cat, who forgave him, and purred. The injection had made her drowsy. She stretched out and went to sleep.

'Keep that abscess open and let it drain,' the Vet said. 'Don't let a scab form.'

The landlord nodded. It wasn't the first abscess the old cat had had, and it wouldn't be the last. She had had more abscesses than she had had kittens.

'There's not an awful lot you can do,' the Vet said, turning to Steven. He poured himself a cup of coffee. His day was not ended yet. Half an hour's breathing space and then a late surgery, which suited country people better. They could bring small animals in for treatment after they had finished their other jobs.

'There must be something.' Foot and mouth was only a rumour in Steven's life, a disease that happened on other farms, but not on his own. There had not been a large epidemic for a good many years and the last one had been before his farming days, and he had not taken much note of it. He vaguely remembered his uncle talking about it, but it was like any other disaster, something that happened to the chap next door, but not to you.

'If it comes near you want to take the cattle in,' the Vet said. 'You ought to have room for most of them inside. Otherwise split the herd into small groups and separate them well. And move any that are near Ken Martin's place. It's as well not to have animals massed too closely.'

'Good job I finished my winter quarters,' Steven said. 'Isn't there anything else we can do?'

'Very little. Use your own feedstuffs if you have them. And don't buy hay from any other farms. If we get it over here you'll have to isolate yourself. But that's not likely. They say it's being contained on the county border. There's no movement of beasts in or out of the area, and the farmers are keeping at home. It's hard on them, but there's no other way to stop it spreading.' The Vet finished his coffee. The door slammed behind him.

'Doesn't do to worry,' the landlord said, stroking his sleepy cat.

'Worry about what?' Ken Martin asked, coming into the room. He was a thin man with a deceptively lazy air about him. In actual fact he was capable of walking any other man off his feet, and could work for hours without tiring. His dark face was usually sombre, but at times amusement lightened it and an irrepressible grin broke over it.

'Foot and mouth,' Steven said. 'The Vet says there are more cases tonight, near the border. I'm going to move my cows away from that far field, well away from yours, Ken.'

'Thought of doing that myself,' Ken Martin said. 'The bigger the gap we can make, the better, I reckon. But it won't spread over here. The outbreaks are usually short and sharp and confined to a single area.'

'Wonder what started it,' Joey said, from the corner of the room. He was still sore about the dead cow. Joey's sorrows were long lasting, and he brooded over his wrongs. When he was brooding he drank and Sarah suffered, and so, sometimes did Steven, as Joey could stay drunk for three days, and in that time he was quite incapable of working. Once Steven had put him to work, but had found him with the tractor rammed into a half-felled tree, sound asleep in the driver's seat. After that Steven coped alone and left the man to recover. He looked at him anxiously now. He had no desire to herd the cattle into winter quarters by himself. It would mean much more work, as they had to be fed instead of grazing for their own food. It was lucky he had plenty of silage as well as hay.

'Funny old germ. Wonder how it starts. Right out of the blue each time,' Joey said. 'Comes and goes, and no one knows how.'

'They reckon it comes from infected swill; meat from the Argentine,' the landlord said. 'At least, that's what my paper says.'

'Carried on hay, straw, human hands and clothes and hair, on feedstuffs, on animal hides, on practically anything you like to mention.' Ken Martin had been reading up everything he could find on the subject, seeking some magic formula that would ensure that if the disease spread his matchless Jerseys would stay free from it. 'It's a damned awful thing.'

'They didn't ought to slaughter,' Joey said. 'In my dad's day we treated the beasts and they got better. There's inoculations for brucellosis. Why don't they inoculate for foot and mouth?'

'Beasts aren't any good when they've had it,' Ken Martin said. 'The milk yield's down. Some of them, in fact most of them, are sterile, maybe for ever, and what good's a barren cow? Or one that gives a low milk yield. And their hooves overgrow and they get very lame. Life's just a burden to them. Besides, if you inoculate you can get carriers, and they say there isn't an inoculation that's really effective for pigs.'

'Damn silly job, farming,' Joey said morosely. Steven looked hard at the landlord and put his thumb down. Joey asked for more beer, but the landlord, deliberately, did not hear him.

'You get swine fever and fowl pest; brucellosis and mastitis; beasts get abscesses and foot rot and foul and horses get strangles and navicular, and damn silly buggers fill your cows with polythene.'

'With polythene?' the landlord said.

'Someone chucked a length over into my cowfield and one of my best cows choked on it. Cows eat some damn silly things,' Steven said.

'One of mine got into the churchyard last year and died of yew poisoning. Some fool went into my field and left the gate open,' Ken Martin said. 'She was a good beast too. It's always the good beasts that suffer, never the non-doer that you'd rather see off the place anyway.'

'This foot and mouth ...' Steven said. 'Every time I see a beast limp I'll be uneasy. It's an awful thing to think about, having every beast on your farm killed and not one left.'

'It's something I'd rather not contemplate,' Ken Martin said. He grinned suddenly. 'It's far enough away. Come on, Steve, cheer up. You'll have us both feeling like Irishmen at a wake and sobbing our sorrows away.'

The door swung open, and the village police sergeant came in.

'I thought I'd find you here,' he said. 'I've just had a phone call from Hinton Netherby. They've got foot and mouth at Nick Carson's place at Lime Tree Walk. Found two pigs with it. They were slaughtering his cattle this afternoon. It's only six miles from here, so I was told to warn you. It may be only an isolated instance, but you can't tell with the beastly thing.'

'But there were no cases nearer than the border,' Jack Martin said.

'They reckon it's coming in on the wind. Blowing straight over to us from the border,' the sergeant said.

'Come on, Joey, we're going to get the cattle in,' Steven said.

'We can get the cattle in. And some of the sheep. But what about the pigs? And the heifers. And the bullocks. Can't wrap them all in disinfectant. It's a hell of a thing,' Joey said passionately, his mind on his beautiful beasts. He was almost disposed to pray, and as the Vicar came in through

56

the doorway he turned to him and spoke impulsively.

'You might pray for our beasts, Vicar.'

'You might, at that,' Ken Martin said, following Joey and Steven out into the night.

The Vicar looked after them, bewildered.

'They've got foot and mouth at Lime Tree Walk, in Hinton Netherby,' the landlord explained.

The Vicar said nothing. There was nothing to say. He had worked too long in a farming community to make light of the disease and he knew as well as anyone the hardship that would be caused on all the farms if the disease struck at Salem Hardacre.

'Six miles away,' the Vicar said.

'And they say its windborne.'

'Could be carried by birds, gulls, or pigeons on farmland; by dogs, foxes, hedgehogs, badgers; rats, weasels, stoats, or even field mice. The birds of the air and the beasts of the field. What do you say to that, Vicar?'

It was Mark Tilley speaking. He had been sitting in the corner unobserved, and was more than half-way drunk.

'It's a wonderul world, isnt it, Vicar? People die, for no good reason, and are born for no good reason. And taken sick for no good reason, and married and given in marriage. And you don't approve of me, do you, Vicar? All because I don't kowtow to convention. Why should I? If I lived in the East it would be convention to have six wives, and if I lived in the time of the Armada it would be convention to denounce my enemies to the Inquisition. And your enemies, Vicar. I think you'd like to do that. The sanctimonious Church. Pray for their beasts, Vicar. That's a laugh, isn't it? As if you would.'

'I'd not only pray for them,' the Vicar said, 'but bless them too. Only today I was over in Hinton Netherby and I'll do the farmers more good by acknowledging modern knowledge and keeping away.'

He turned and walked out into the lane, and behind him Mark Tilley looked at the inkeeper and then shrugged.

'Bully for the parson,' he said.

The Master came in through the doorway.

'And bully for the squire.' He went out, singing under his breath.

'I can't bear that young man,' the Master said. 'Where is everybody tonight?'

'Steven Fenn and Joey and Ken Martin were here earlier, but the police sergeant called to say there was foot and mouth at Hinton Netherby. They slaughtered at Lime Tree Walk today.'

'My God!' the Master said. 'Give me a pint, quick, now I'm here, and then I'm off. Poor old Nick Carson. What a hell of a thing. Better go and look at the sheep. You never know. My God! What a thing to happen!'

He drained his mug in record time and went out into the night, hurrying down the lane past Hollow End. All the lights were on in the yard and the dogs were herding the bewildered cows who could not understand why they were being brought in at such a strange hour, and who remained provokingly unco-operative. The farm was noisy with beasts, the cattle lowing, the dogs barking, the hens clucking from inside the henhouse, the jenny donkey adding her bray to the din.

'God help us all,' said the Master, as he hurried by, and if they had heard him Steven and Joey would have echoed his words.

CHAPTER SIX

THREE days later beasts were killed at three more farms in the county. The farmers isolated themselves, tying up the gates, and putting the official notices on them.

KEEP OUT. INFECTED AREA. FOOT AND MOUTH DISEASE.

No one was welcome. Sarah masked the notice that advertised potatoes, eggs, and dressed chickens, and Joey laid a deep mat of straw both inside and outside the gates and at the far end of the lane, soaking them in disinfectant. He washed his boots before he came back to the farm.

Luckily there was little time to brood during the day. The work seemed endless. Joey took feed to the cattle, and washed them down and milked alone, while Steven began to work out the amounts of silage and hay and extra feed needed for each cow.

'We'll run out long before winter's ended at this rate,' he said morosely, and rang up to make arrangements for extra deliveries, stressing that he did not want the lorries on his premises. They could unload in the lane on to his own trailers.

'Gulls everywhere,' Sarah said, having fed the chickens, and the pigs. 'Supposing they bring it in? And I'm boiling the pig swill for two hours today. Can't be too careful.'

Can't be too careful became the rule of the day. Steven examined every beast on the place and found himself morbidly washing his hands over and over again, as if the very act held some kind of magic in it.

It was not easy to look over the heifers. They were skittish and did not stand still and were apt to push and butt. And the bullocks were awkward, not used to being herded by the cattle dog both morning and evening. They shied away.

'Soon see if they're off song by their behaviour,' Joey said. He was growing morose. There was too much work to do and too much worry, and all his and Sarah's savings were tied up in those bullocks. You got compensation, but that wouldn't be the top market price, and they had little enough to spare in the way of hard cash for their old age. Not the sort of thing you thought of happening even though you knew about it.

Steven seemed to have lost his energy.

There were so many beasts to examine and so many minor ills that might afflict them. Foot rot in the sheep ... suppose it wasn't foot-rot but a mild case of foot and mouth? And could you have a mild case that you might not recognize but that might infect the others? And suppose you got a beast carrying it without symptoms? And if the sheep were in the furthermost field and the cows got it, would the sheep be far enough away, or would they have to be slaughtered? He and Joey ought to divide jobs ... one of them look after the sheep and the other the cattle and keep out of each other's road. But it wasn't possible. Not with all the work on the farm, and the extra feeding, and the mucking out, and one hundred and eighty beasts to milk. And not only milk, but the cows to wash down first. And churns to scald and the parlour to clean, and the yard to hose. Steven ordered gallons of the best disinfectant he could find, badgering three vets before he was finally satisfied. His scientific training helped here, and his knowledge of the various techniques used in industry in ensuring sterility for various biochemical processes.

The focal point of each day was the farming bulletin. As the days went by, the news became more and more grim. Thirty cases and over eight thousand beasts slaughtered. The next day's toll went up to thirty-six cases. Thirty-six farms where all the beasts had died. Thirty-six farms with no income from milk, no income from cattle to be sold in the coming beast sales. Thirty-six more farms where next year there would be no wool, no lambs for the spring market, no in-calf heifers, no calves, no cows. No chance of making a few pounds by selling a pig or a bullock. And nothing to do. That must be the worst. Isolated in the deserted yard, unable to find a job worth tackling, without a beast in sight.

None of them had a word to say as they watched; by the end of the fourth week the figures were unimaginable. The waste of livestock was sickening to contemplate and it was as well not even to try and imagine how the farmers felt. Or their wives. Or the children. Steven knew of two farms where the children cried when the beasts went to market. How did you keep them out of the way when every beast on the farm had to die and the pyre of cremation stank the whole place out? News flashes of slaughtered cows and burning pyres began to be almost commonplace. At night dreams took over. Dreams of cattle dying, of tormented beasts unable to understand what was happening, of Shala lying dead, her hooves rigid, her eyes staring at the sky. He lay awake listening to the sounds from the byre. Was that a beast coughing, or a cow lowing in pain? Was Pet just oozing spittle from her cud, or was she starting the awful salivation that acompanied the disease?

The nights were endless. Bess often watched, puzzled, as her master paced the room and finally dressed long before milking and went downstairs to sit with the teapot in front of him, and the empty cup which he had forgotten to fill, and then went out into the icy wind before dawn and listened to the sounds from the sheep field, looked at the heifers and bullocks and walked through the cattle sheds where the cows waited drowsily for milking time.

It was relief to turn to the horses. Mick and Grey were groomed until they shone, and often Steven walked them round and round the yard, not being anxious to have them in the fields, lest bird or badger or fox or passing hare or roving dog had brought the germ, and it lay hidden in his grass, to come across the yard on a shod hoof, lying in wait for the cattle as they walked out of the shed and into the milking parlour, lying in wait to infect and spread until the beasts began to ail and the whole sickening system had to be invoked.

His only contact with the outside world was the telephone and an occasional shouted conversation over the gate. He and Sarah and Joey rarely spoke. There was nothing to say, and Joey was morose, and, Steven suspected, spent the free hour at night drinking. Sarah, like himself, was becoming obsessed by the need for cleanliness. She boiled the swill for far longer than was needed, she washed her hands and changed her apron before going near the cattle, and she nagged at Joey until he too was more than usually clean. The dairy was scoured and scrubbed and stank of disinfectant and the straw mats in the yard were laced afresh several times a day.

Ken Martin, telephoning one morning, sounded as if he too was feeling the strain.

'Mollie's taken all the precautions anyone can think of and a few that she must have invented,' he said. 'We've sacks of onions in the place, onions spread round the fields and byres, onions everywhere. We'll stink of them for months. Mollie says they'll trap germs. And we're giving the cattle borax drenches. It seems like magic to me, and I suggested she put up some mountain ash and a few horseshoes. Best to let women have their way. Life gets mighty uncomfortable if they don't.'

So Ken was still all right. Steven went out to ask Joey about borax drenches, but Joey was in the deserted cattle field with the shotgun. The hare was pelting along the hedge. Joey sighted and shot, and she kicked convulsively and died.

'She could carry the germ,' he said. 'I'm burning her body. And we ought to kill that stag if we see him. He goes to all the farms for hay.'

By the end of the fifth week of isolation everyone was numb. It was only possible to live from hour to hour, from day to day, thankful that there was enough work to carry through from dawn until long after dark, that the cattle needed milking and feeding and the horses grooming and exercising. That there was mucking out to do, and the animals to look over, and that the beasts at least were untouched by fear. Shala still expected Joey to bring her her bread, and Mick and Grey demanded attention and the little jenny wanted her share too, especially as her foal was almost due. And it was nearly time for Bess's pups. There was no end to the work.

Steven slept now at night, too exhausted to worry. At times he woke, bedevilled by nightmares but as the days went by and nothing happened and the disease moved away from the village, he began to relax. Sarah took extra trouble in preparing tasty meals, and Joey was less morose, although he had insisted in lying in wait for the stag and despatching him with Steven's rifle.

'Poor old brute. He wasn't long for this world, anyway,' Joey said as they looked at the gaunt carcase. The antlers were only an echo of former glory, the ribs protruded through the mangy hide, and the gaping mouth revealed that the animal had almost no teeth and had almost starved to death because he was unable to feed properly. Joey buried him in quicklime in the sour patch of field that they had never been able to cultivate, down at the corner of the lane.

It was the man who collected the churns who told them that the disease had struck again in the village, this time on Ed Lucas's small farm. All his beasts had been slaughtered the day before. He had the land to the east of the Master.

Steven looked at Joey.

'Of all the damned bad luck,' he said.

Joey went indoors. When he came out a few minutes later he stank of whisky.

'Can't you hide it from him?' Steven asked Sarah irritably an hour later, when Joey had spilt two buckets of disinfectant, fallen twice in the midden, and managed to produce a spate of some of the richest language Steven had ever heard.

'Reckon he got at your whisky. He hasn't any,' Sarah said. 'I put the other bottles away just now. Didn't think he'd do a thing like that.'

'It's getting us all down, Sarah,' Steven said heavily. It was a good job drinking didn't appeal to him. It was one way of release. But not for him. His only release lay in work. He began to muck out the jenny donkey's stall, and then took the whitewash and put a quite unnecessary extra coat

63

on the inside of the foaling room. He wanted to be sure that everywhere was free from germs.

Christmas came and went. There seemed little point in feasting but Sarah made a traditional meal and served it on a table decorated with holly. Steven was inclined to eye even that with dread. It might have the virus on its leaves, blown on the wind from Ed Lucas's place, but he said nothing, and they ended with the brandy that he kept for special occasions, and went back to the chores that seemed to mount daily. When the lorry came to pick up the churns that afternoon they heard that a small farm six miles away had spent Christmas Day slaughtering. That night Joey found one of the bottles of whisky and drank himself into a stupor. Sarah helped with the milking in the morning, her face grim.

'Boxing Day,' Steven said. It was a mockery. He did not know the man whose beasts had died, but his thoughts were with him. He pushed the hair back out of his eyes. Hair and beard needed cutting, and perhaps Sarah could cope later, but just now there were all Joey's jobs to do, and he and Sarah had enough without the extra work. Sarah gave Shala her bread and when she turned away there were tears in her eyes. Steven did not comment. They were all under too great a strain.

He went outside and looked at the fields, which were winter bleak enough, heaven knew, without being deserted too. Both cowfields were empty. The sheep grazed the third field, and the bullocks and heifers were still outside, but almost out of sight beyond the hedge. It was time to go and look at them again. One of the cows had mastitis, and was slightly off her feed. He had been bothered at first but the symptoms were plain. There was always at least one beast suffering from the disease. It was a nuisance as she had to be treated with antibiotics and the milk had to be kept separate. It meant hand milking, which was simplest as then he did not have to worry about infected milking cups and extra careful sterilization, and also he could gauge how bad she was. And one of the sheep had cut its eye on barbed wire. The cut needed dressing.

He walked idly over to the sheep field. The beasts were

fat and in good condition. Their fleeces were thick with winter growth, and they were lively enough. He whistled to the sheepdogs and they came to him, and he sent them round the ewes. It was quicker when Joey was there to take half the flock but no use bothering about that. He sighed with relief as he finished the first field. No sign of trouble there.

He watched the bigger dog bringing the sheep to him, and then his heart almost stopped. One of the beasts was limping. Not a small limp, dear God, but an almighty big one that threatened to throw her at every step. They couldn't have overlooked foot rot and the animals went through footbaths twice a month since the infection had started. Steven sent the smaller dog to single her and bring her to him, and went to meet them, his heart thudding, his mouth dry with fear. Every beast would have to go. It wasn't fair. After all his work.

He was almost level with the sheep. It was a terrible limp. He went to her, and relief flooded him, leaving him weak. She had yards of fine nylon line wrapped round both front legs. Some idiot must have been fishing in the brook, and got his line tangled and left it behind. Nuisance enough, but not half as bad as he'd feared. He was so relieved that he whistled as he cut the line from her legs, and sent her off happily with a slap across the rump. The lameness passed. She joined the flock, apparently none the worse. Sarah wondered at his cheerfulness, for he continued to whistle as he hosed down the yard, and gave Shala an extra piece of bread, and took carrots and apples to the jenny and Mick and Grey, and for the first time for weeks threw a stick for Bob, and played a game of ball with Bess.

That night there were only ten new cases of foot and mouth reported in the whole county. The disease was waning. They would be all right after all. Steven went to bed early, and, for the first time for weeks, overslept, so that Sarah had to wake him at milking time. Joey was already in the cow shed, but he was still morose. He said nothing to Steven, and Steven, although he had meant to read a riot act, found that he could not be bothered. When Joey got upset then Jocy drank. It was as simple as that, and maybe better to let him alone than try and stop him. He might take to worse vices, or beat Sarah, or even go out of his mind. What was a bit of drinking now and again?

'Found a sheep limping yesterday,' Steven said, 'it gave me a turn, but it was only nylon line round her legs. Thank goodness.'

'Just as well,' Joey said. It wasn't much of a response, but at least he was normal again. Steven went to muck out the stables and walk the horses. Joey was not fond of horses, and Mick and Grey knew it and played him up. Mick would give a weird and evil little grin and bend his head and nip Joey's hand, and Grey was not above standing on the cowman's foot, just to show him who was boss. And it wasn't Joey.

CHAPTER SEVEN

THE Grey Goose was a strange and empty place at night, and Herbert found it sad. It was bad enough to drive along the lanes on his way to town and see the shut gates and the notices, the pads of straw soaked in disinfectant, the men who normally welcomed him waving from a safe distance, the women with set faces. Mollie Martin was having treatment for nerves, and not surprising. She woke at night crying, unable to stop, and the doctor had sent her some sleeping tablets. And Ed Lucas leaned on his gate with his peregrine on his wrist, looking like a lost soul. He hadn't had many beasts, but he had a way with animals and his were all pets. Compensation couldn't make up for that.

The Vicar came in every night for the pint of bitter that he enjoyed so much. He could no longer play chess with the Master, but surprisingly, Mark Tilley had offered to play instead, and proved a good player. When he was not trying to impress other people, he was likeable, even if he did sometimes drink too much and was not married, or so they said, to the girl who lived in his cottage with him.

Robbie Preston came in from time to time. He was supposed to be reporting on the epidemic and he had produced three very harrowing articles for his paper, but now too many of his friends were affected and he could no longer write his copy. Everything annoyed him, from the policy instituted by the Government, to the soothing words issued at times by various minor officials and some major ones. From the way in which so many other things were affected and so many were suffering. Racing was stopped, and there were jockeys out of pocket as well as all the other people ... the betting shops and the men who earned a living on the fringe of racing. No hunting. No shooting. No fishing. No mass gatherings, but they let football go on and Robbie didn't approve of that. Where there were people there was danger to beasts. People carried the disease on their clothes. And there were people who went from farm to farm to watch the slaughter. Good job he didn't carry a gun, Robbie thought. He imagined himself shooting the gawping fools. He hated them all, the people who made capital out of other people's misfortunes. He had had good money paid for his articles, but he had sent it to the N.F.U. with a request that it be used for research into the spread of the virus and how to combat the disease.

'They need to do more research,' he said, pursuing his own line of thought.

'Not much point in spending money on research if the official policy is a slaughter policy,' Mark Tilley pointed out, and added 'check' as he moved his queen to threaten his opponent's king.

The Vicar moved a bishop.

'Slaughter might not always work,' Robbie said. 'No one really knows how the disease got here this time. No source of infection has been found. How do we know it's not endemic? It crops up in one place or another every year, doesn't it? Might lie in the ground for all we know, like the anthrax virus. That can lie dormant for ten years and suddenly become active again. No one knows much about viruses. They can't multiply outside a living body, but they can live on outside it, and become active again when some creature picks them up. It's daft. They need to find out more, much more, not just say glibly that the disease can be contained and the slaughter policy is best. They ought to make a barrier of inoculated animals all round the infected area. They ought to find a decent vaccine. They ought to find out how the beastly thing's being spread.'

'My brother's a farmer,' Mark Tilley said. He took a pawn with his knight. The Vicar smiled and took the knight. 'Damn! My brother says that if he could import cattle from Europe and inoculate, he could have a foot-and-mouth-immune herd in five years. Then there'd be no need for everyone to live like this. The edge of the abyss!'

The Vicar looked at him curiously. He was learning some unexpected things about Mark Tilley. Not half as much of a rebel as he pretended. He moved his own queen.

'Checkmate!'

Mark looked at the board carefully.

'It is, too,' he said. 'I'll stand you another half pint, Vicar.'

The landlord set two mugs upon the bar counter, and Mark paid, and returned to his place at the table. There was a sketch pad beside it, and he leaned back and began to draw the cat, who was lying by the fire, her body extended, so that she could enjoy the blaze.

'It's hard to know what is the right and what the wrong of it all,' the Vicar said. 'It's a desperate measure at the best of times, everybody knows that. And the officials know it too. After all, many of them are farmers, and have farms of their own, and at least two of the higher officials have been hit by the plague.'

'It must be harder for the smaller men,' the landlord said. 'No money in the bank and no leeway. It must have been a lean Christmas for a good many.' It did not occur to him to mention that a hamper of drink had gone, at his own expense, to Ed Lucas, and to the other three farmers that he knew. Or that among the bottles were chocolates for the children and bottles of scent for the women on the farms.

'It's hard for everyone,' Robbie said. 'Like throwing a stone in a pool and seeing the ripples widen. There are farms with no work for the men, and they can either lose their hands, or find money to pay them. There's a man I know who's just started up with a ruddy great loan from the bank. He's lost every penny, and the compensation will just about pay off the interest. Then he's got to re-stock, and start again, and it's not going to be possible. His farm's going up for auction. Saved up for fifteen years, been there for six months, and now look at him, finished.'

'Doesn't make a man believe in your God, Vicar,' Mark Tilley said. 'Or are you going to tell us that the ways of the Lord are inscrutable?'

'I sometimes find the ways of the Lord very hard to understand myself,' the Vicar answered. He lifted one of the kittens that was playing with his shoelace. 'I think perhaps it pays in this life to be content with very little. That's why women are often so much more resilient than men. They can gain immense pleasure from such small things; from a kitten playing with a straw, or a rose blooming in the rain. From the first spring lambs, or the sight of a child asleep. Most women are happy with far less than most men. Some have ambition, but not always for the things men hanker for. Some are mercenary, but not as many as you'd think. And even the most mercenary is more likely to have her heart enthralled by a puppy than by a diamond bracelet.'

'What shall it profit a man if he gain the whole world and lose all his possessions,' Robbie said. 'And women, you think, Vicar, have souls?'

'Why shouldn't they?' the Vicar asked in astonishment.

'I wanted to see your reaction,' Robbie said. 'I was the sort of little boy that pulled legs off flies to see if they minded.'

'I doubt that, too,' the Vicar said. He put the kitten down, and stretched himself, and stood up, a tall lean man, with dark eyes that seemed to see visions, and a streak of absent-minded unworldliness in his make-up. An unworldliness that led him into forgetting the time when music was playing, but that never prevented him from being where he was most needed, or from judging a man correctly. His wife had died some months before, and he found the parish tiring on his own, the more so now, when he wanted to comfort those who were isolated, and could do no more than telephone them, lest he too became a carrier of the disease.

The Vicar stood for a moment looking out of the window at the night. The village street was cosy with lights in the windows of the old almshouses; the lamps outside the church gleamed on one of the stained glass windows. A tree was illuminated from underneath and the bare branches glistened with faint frosting. It was a cold evening. Nothing was changed.

'Plague over England,' the Vicar said, his voice musing. 'I wonder what it was like in the old days, when plague came to men and women and children and they shut themselves in their homes, and some of them died there. And yet the plague passed. People survived, life went on, and now it seems impossible that such a thing should ever have happened.'

'Do you know the old plague village on the hill?' Mark Tilley asked.

The Vicar nodded.

'On the hill?' Robbie said, lifting his head from inspecting a damp patch on the table with an intensity that was out of all proportion to the significance of the mark.

'The ruins on the hill. The foundations of a church, the broken walls of forsaken cottages. The old village was up there, in the days of the Great Plague. Men ran from it. The people died, and the houses were burned by the returning villagers. They built the new village and the new church, and erected a stone in the church to those who died of plague. It's in the Lady Chapel. Almost unreadable now. I often wonder what it was like for those who were left up there to die.' The Vicar enjoyed reading the history of his parish.

'The trees grew up and shaded the ruins, and the leaves whispered. And by night strange shapes cried among the branches, and the trees bowed down to the ground, and a haze drifted among them, a haze that was fog, that was smoke, that was the wraith of human forms. And by day the jays screamed, and by night the owls mourned, and no man dared set foot on the hill. For the old village was a haunted place and those who had died knew no rest, nor would, for all eternity.'

Mark had spoken almost as if he were dreaming.

'Well, well,' the landlord said and began to polish a glass vigorously. Robbie stared at the artist out of his tired blue eyes, but did not voice his thoughts.

'Who wrote that?' the Vicar asked as they walked out into the road, where dead leaves rustled in the gutter.

'Sue. The girl who lives with me. Oh dammit, Vicar, we're married properly, marriage lines and all, but I like contributing to the stories of immoral artists. People seem to expect it of one.'

'I knew you were married,' the Vicar said equably.

71

'Who told you?'

'Susan herself. She thought it would relieve my mind, but asked me not to spread the word around, as it would upset you. You liked to be thought unconventional. But she didn't. Have you never thought about that?'

'She didn't say she minded,' Mark said.

'It started as a game, I expect,' the Vicar agreed. 'But women are very cruel and Susan is being ostracized, for no fault of hers. And she's a friendly soul. She often slips in to see me and to chat to Mrs. Roach, who does for me. In more ways than one,' he added, with a rueful smile. Mrs. Roach was a managing woman.

'Then you'd better come in and let us return your hospitality.' Mark pushed open the wooden gate and marched the two steps across the garden to the front door. He pushed it open.

'Sue? Are you up? We have a visitor.'

Startled, Susan came to the door. She was small and slim, blonde hair cascading over her shoulders. She smiled up at the Vicar.

'Come and share our cocoa.'

The tiny living room was warm, the fire blazing, bright rugs and curtains and cushions contrasting with whitewashed walls and scrubbed stone floor. There was very little furniture, but what there was looked pleasant, and went well with the cottage. Susan had been writing. A scribbling pad lay on the floor where she had dropped it. A magnificent copper coloured Persian cat was lying on the hearth, his expression haughty. He lifted a regal head to stare at the newcomer.

'Robbie loves him,' Susan said.

'Does he come here?' the Vicar asked.

'Often. He just sits and holds the cat, and sometimes talks a little. I think it makes him feel at home. He lives in beastly digs.' Susan was pouring cocoa from a brown earthenware jug into three bright scarlet pottery mugs.

'Steven Fenn calls in, and the Master often comes to give me advice about my horse,' Mark said. 'All men,' he added. The thought had not occurred to him before.

72

'The women don't approve of my morals,' Susan said.

'Then it's time we told them you are an honest woman,' Mark answered. 'Why didn't you tell me, Sue? That none of the women would have anything to do with you. Beastly old bitches,' he added venomously.

'Some of them do. Mollie Martin comes sometimes, but she doesn't tell anyone in case Jill gets to hear she visits me. It might give Jill ideas. She's only sixteen. After all, they all have daughters. Would you let your daughter live in sin?'

'Over my dead body,' Mark said, without thinking, and then caught the glance that Susan exchanged with the Vicar and began to laugh. 'O.K. O.K. You win!'

'I'll tell Mrs. Roach in the morning that it's all been a misunderstanding. Everyone will know before lunch time,' the Vicar said. 'You didn't tell me what you were quoting just now,' he added. 'About the plague village.'

'Sue,' Mark said. 'She's writing a book about the legends in this part of the world. There are dozens of them. There's the ghost at Hollow End, where the boy was killed by a bull, and there's a ghost in your churchyard, did you know, Vicar?'

'The woman who walks under the Witching Elm,' the Vicar said. 'She was suspected of being a witch so she was thrown into the manor lake to see if she would float and she drowned. They buried her under the elm, but she has never stayed in her grave. And there's the suicide that was buried at the cross roads, and the man who hanged himself in Ed Lucas's old barn.'

'Did you make the last two up?' Susan asked suspiciously.

The Vicar shook his head.

'My predecessors kept diaries. You must come and look at them. Personally, the only ghost I ever saw was unfortunately only too real. It proved to be one of Ken Martin's cows, and she had eaten enough yew to kill her by the time I found her. If I'd come home an hour earlier I could have prevented her. I often think her ghost should haunt me for not coming home in time.'

'Show him the drawings you're doing for the book,' Susan said.

73

Mark's studio was a converted loft. The whole of one side of the roof had been removed and covered with glass. Moonlight flirted with metal in dark corners and glinted on the floor, until Steven switched on the light.

There was a big portfolio of drawings on the table. Steven leafed through them, and suddenly the Vicar found himself looking at the ruined plague village, the trees that sheltered it bending eerily together, while wraiths of smoke drifted from the ground and the place brooded.

On the next page a giant bull, ecstatic with rage, was charging a boy who ran towards the onlookers, his face contorted with panic. In a moment the bull would explode into fury, and the boy lie dead.

'What else do you draw?' the Vicar asked.

Mark turned the pages. Cattle of every sort jumped out of them; Jersey heifers and Friesian bulls, an impressive shorthorn bull, Bob the Labrador, standing, looking up at his master, his eyes ardent; a fox chasing through bracken, an otter diving cleanly into water, a bird on a twig, Ed Lucas and his peregrine.

'I illustrate farming books,' Mark said. 'My father had a farm, but he died, and my mother couldn't manage it and sold it to send me to school. I didn't want to go back to farming, and I found I could draw, and that I could draw animals best. I always lived in the country. I hunted, and that's why I keep old Tyrant. I oughtn't to, I can't afford him, but he gives us exercise, and he's fun to teach. I can teach him things I can't teach any other horse. Him and me, we're a team. Buddies. Empathy or something. I don't know. If we can't earn money any other way we can always join a circus.'

'Othello's occupation's gone,' the Vicar said, suddenly, realizing why Mark had been hanging aimlessly around the village for the past few weeks. 'No beasts to draw?'

'That's right. I have to draw from life or it won't come right. I'm one of the minor casualties of the epidemic. We live a bit hand to mouth, Sue and me. But we'll get by.'

The Vicar found himself wishing he had been more perceptive. He would see that the village heard about this and there would be a change in their attitude towards Sue. And the villagers could send food in as recompense, and as wedding presents. The verger had beehives, and sold honey. He could start the ball rolling. And Mrs. Roach could bake some bread. And the grocer could give a hamper.

It was a relief to be able to plan, instead of contemplating the desolate fields and the stricken farms, and the sight of Ed Lucas leaning on his gate looking as if life held nothing for him any more.

CHAPTER EIGHT

THE jenny foal was born the day that they slaughtered the sheep on Jack Dodd's farm. The virus had apparently left the area, and long sighs of relief were drawn by everyone. Then, after more than a week had passed, a dying sheep was found in the field near the Vicarage garden. The Vicar saw the beast first. He went to look at her, not realizing what was wrong. The signs were only too plain and he went to the telephone. Jack swore.

'Must be the old ewe who's been under the weather off and on all year,' he said morosely. 'I shouldn't have kept her. In fact, I wouldn't have done if it hadn't been for the epidemic. She'd have gone to the sales eight weeks ago.'

'It might not be foot and mouth,' the Vicar said. 'I'm no expert.'

'It sounds like it. And, Vicar, sounds as if you were close enough to need to isolate yourself. Where is she?'

'Right beside my hedge,' the Vicar said. 'And my dog's been in the field too. He slipped out this morning and went through the hedge. He came back as soon as I called him, but he was in that field.'

'It sounds as if you'll have to get a locum, or shut the church,' Jack said. 'And keep your dog inside, or he'll be for the high jump too.'

He rang off. When the Vicar next looked out of his study window the dogs were busy rounding up the herd. Jack had been unable to separate the beasts into small flocks, as he had not sufficient land. The woolly backs packed solid. The field was vibrant with noise; sheep bleated, dogs barked, and both Jack and his shepherd were whistling.

'Come now, Bet. Come now, Lad. Come on, then, good dog.'

The calls continued. The Vicar sighed as he saw the pens being erected. It would be quicker to mass the sheep and kill them. There would be panic among the poor beasts. There would be no flocks for these shepherds to watch tomorrow.

Joey, cresting the little hill that afternoon to look over his own flock, saw the smoke in the distance. He went back to the farm.

'There's smoke at Jack Dodds' place,' he said heavily.

Steven went to the telephone. The Vicar would know. He listened, and his heart was pounding when he put the receiver down again. He nodded.

'Not so bad for Jack as for some,' Joey said. 'He hasn't bred his sheep and they'd be sold at next sale anyway. Maybe drop a bit in price, that's all. Good job he's got the beagles to occupy him.'

'It's still a waste,' Steven said.

It was one thing to have the beasts used for meat, another to have every one of them killed senselessly and flung to the flames. And how far was Jack from him? Suppose rats brought it to him? Less than a mile and they shared a boundary on Eagle Hill . . . and it might come in on the wind . . .

That night Steven could not eat, and Joey found another of the whisky bottles hidden in the barn. Sarah hid the last two elsewhere, and did Joey's jobs with a set face, unwilling to speak lest her tongue betrayed her. She found herself, irrationally, wishing that Steven would drink, or that he had some means of relief that would take the taut look from his face and the stricken expression from his eyes. She went out to the jenny donkey and sat in the dark stable and nursed the foal, chiding herself for idiocy. If they caught the bug from Jack Dodds, then at least they'd have the donkeys and the horses left, and the foal was a symbol, although she did not know why.

That evening Steven did not sit on the tree trunk. It was cold, and there was a fog in the air, fog made thicker by the burning beasts, fog made potent by the stench in the air, fog made fearful by the knowledge of death.

The frost bit at cheeks and fingers and Bess followed unhappily. Only a few days now before her pups were born. Her paws were cold, and she lifted them high, as if that would help warm them and delay contact with the icy ground.

Steven went to the sheep field. The warm woolly bodies were lying on the ground. They were sleepy and lazy, huddled together for warmth, lying against hedge and bank and tree, sheltering from frost and wind. He had taken the first batch of ewes into the lambing shed. In a few days the first one should start by producing twins. It was a good job he had his own rams, and had been able to use them when regulations clamped down. Many of the sheep farmers had been unable to bring the rams to the sheep and their flocks would be barren.

He watched them, enjoying the sight of the plump well-fed bodies, the placid heads that lifted and looked incuriously at him.

They knew Bess was no sheep dog, and she was sitting quietly beside her master, waiting for him to go. She wanted to lie by the warm fire. She put out a paw and scraped his leg and whimpered.

'All right, old girl,' Steven said, suddenly aware of the bitter wind and the ache of ears and fingers. He had a headache and a shivery feeling and was more tired than he had ever been in his life. He hoped he wasn't starting flu. How could he, when he was there alone and had seen no one? But people passed the gate and food was brought to the farm, and the germ might lie on bread or on fruit ... and the foot and mouth virus might come that way as well. Or perhaps the men who disinfected the farms carried the virus in their hair, or in their mouths? Might it not lie in a human carrier in nose or nails or teeth crevices, doing him no harm but waiting to attack a beast?

Or might men not have it in the form of a cold and the germ change and mutate to something else in sheep and cattle? Might he not have already poisoned his own beasts? He thought unhappily of the way a chicken pox virus could change and become shingles. Suppose other things could do that too? It was as fantastic as science fiction, but much more frightening. He wanted to put a mask over his face when he milked the cattle, to make Joey and Sarah mask themselves too, to ensure that everything was safe, germ-free, sterile.

The cattle were dreaming. Shala looked up and licked his hand, and he wondered muzzily if that might not have germs on it, and looked at it under the light as if expecting to see some sign. He shut the cows in, and went across to the farmhouse, and Bess voiced a deep sigh of relief and flopped heavily on to the mat by the fire.

Steven did not want a milk drink. He made tea. He felt odd, slightly light-headed, a little shivery, he longed for bed, yet knew he could not rest. The silent farmhouse was an abomination. No one else in any room, no one to speak to, no one he dared telephone at this time of night. No one who could care if his farm stayed clean or caught the plague. Plague over England. Was this how men felt in the old days when they hid themselves away from the world with leprosy? Unclean. Unclean. And the handbell tolled its dreadful message and people ran. Today there was no handbell. Only a notice that said KEEP OUT. And if the plague struck there were the men who came, the police guards, and the ministry executioners. Plague over England.

Bess licked his hand, knowing he was unhappy, and he sat with his leg pressed against her warm body. Black Cat and Tom Cat were both confined to the house, as they foraged after rats on too many farms. They objected strongly. Tom Cat would probably have to be locked in an outhouse as he was wrecking the covers of the chairs, but Black Cat was enjoying unusual warmth, and milk to steal, as Sarah was not used to locking food up out of the cats' reach. They would both be fat and lazy when they were allowed to go free. One of Black Cat's kittens jumped on to Steven's lap and purred throatily, achieving brief Paradise.

It was no use going to bed. He could not bear the thought of the empty silent room, or even face the effort of climbing the stairs. He made up the fire, and pulled the big settee close to it, and stretched out, to endure nightmares that terrified him, and that grew progressively worse, until he woke shivering, knowing that there were no animals left on his farm, that outside in the silent night the byres were empty and the sheep were gone, and that he was too old and too ill to start again. He would sell the farm and go away and live cooped up in some horrible flat, and die too soon because there was nothing left to keep him alive.

An owl hooted and one of the cattle lowed, and Steven sat up, throwing off the dream. It was cold, and he flung more fuel on the fire and put the kettle on. A knock came at the back door and he looked at it, startled, wondering who on earth could be outside in the night.

He opened it, and found Sarah, fully dressed.

'I thought you might be ill. I saw the light downstairs for ever so long,' she said.

'Touch of flu.' Steven was unable to tell her how pleased he was to see her, to have her fussing and grumbling about him, making up the fire again, and bringing blankets from his bed and a pillow so that he could settle on the big couch, as if she knew the terrors that awaited him upstairs in the dark. She brought the tea, and went out into the night to return with the whisky bottle. She poured a generous quantity into the cup.

'You drink that,' she said. 'Pity we can't dose the cattle with it. Keeps away a power of ills.'

It brought warmth and relaxation. Steven began to doze, and was sleeping quietly when Sarah left, and returned to her own bed to lie awake in her turn and confront her own private demons. The farm was her life. She had lived in that cottage since she was born, and every beast was as familiar to her as if she had bred it herself. Also she was worried about the two men. Men hadn't the resilience of women. Joey took to drink, and might get worse, much worse, if the plague hit their farm, and Mr. Fenn wasn't a young man and he looked wretched tonight and it might be the flu but it was made worse by worry and he had poured all his time and money and pride into Hollow End. And he'd waited long enough to come to the farm, the Lord knew.

80

Her thoughts drifted back to Steven when he was a young man, and she had been herself about sixteen. He had been part of the farm for all the years of her life, but that year he had been ill and come to spend six months with his uncle and aunt and then she had realized how much it meant to him. It had seemed a shame that his mother insisted he took some other job. Parents shouldn't be allowed to choose for their children, she thought.

She was still awake when the alarm clock told her it was milking time. She roused Joey, who dressed, grumbling, and together they went out into the freezing dark where there was not even a hint of dawn. Steven was still asleep, and she left him, and went to help her husband with the cattle, washing them down gently, revelling in the feel of warm hides beneath her hand, in the toss of an impatient head, in the warm lick from Shala's tongue, acknowledging, as she always did, the humans who tended her, and made her comfortable, and fed her. Joey gave the cow her crust, and then set to milking, and the song of the machines was the first thing that Steven heard when he woke, to find Bess licking his face and the day emerging from the darkness, pale, cold, and unwelcoming.

He felt better, and, seeing that milking was almost ended, he shaved, and changed his shirt, Shaving did not take long, as most of his face was bearded, and by the time Joey and Sarah had finished he had bacon cooking in the pan and eggs waiting to be broken and a pot full of strong tea, and the bread cut ready. Sarah had done his job, so there was no reason why he should not do hers.

She insisted on dosing him with aspirin, and persuaded him to spend most of his time indoors, but it was not long before he was fretting. Joey had too much to do, and Sarah couldn't do all his share and her own, and he wanted to look at the sheep, to make sure that no beast was sick, that no hidden horror waited for him today. He had thought the danger ended, and its return had been a second shock, greater than the first, and all the suspense had to be lived through again, and he had no energy left to contend with the fears that beset him.

At last he put on his thick greatcoat and his hat and took a stick and whistled to Bess, who came reluctantly. She hated the cold ground beneath her, and the sting of the wind in her eyes, and would have liked to stay by the fire, but she would not leave Steven.

There was a movement by the haystack. Bob had been locked in the kennel since the disease broke out, to keep him from wandering, as he was liable to run off if there was a bitch in season on any farm within a quite incredible radius. He had barked once in the night, and then dropped nose on paws, and growled softly, sure he had heard a noise, but discouraged because he was locked up. He barked again, but it was only the prowling fox, bent on his own affairs, wanting to make up for a fruitless night by catching a rat or two behind the stacks.

Bess growled, and then ran forward, her nose eager. Steven followed her, puzzled. She began to whine, sniffing at the edge of the haystack. Steven kicked at the hay, and was horrified when he was answered by a hoarse voice. He bent forward and dragged hay off the man who was hiding in the stack, and was even more appalled to see he had a woman with him.

They crawled out. They were covered in straw but even at the best of times they could not have been tidy. Both wore the discarded remnants of other people, clothes that would have disgraced a scarecrow, the man in a tattered coat and an array of filthy scarves, a thin covering of fox red hair over his scraggy face, a puny beard brushing his scrawny neck, his feet in boots that did not fit, in boots that were far better than the rest of his clothes, and that made his spindly legs look outsize.

The woman had grey hair that escaped from a dirty scarf bound round her head. There was an odd light in her blue eyes, and she began to wheedle in a miserable singsong voice.

'What the bloody hell are you doing on my land?' Steven roared.

Terror had overtaken him. They had no right to be here, and God knew what farm they had been on before, on what land they had walked with their idiot feet, or what fields they had passed through.

Sarah heard his voice and came running.

'Heaven help us,' she said faintly, when she saw the couple. 'You'll not get much sense out of them. It's Idiot Mac and Batty Betty, and neither have as much gump as one of my old hens.'

Mac began to giggle.

'Slept in hay,' he said. 'Warm in hay. Mac and Betty always sleep in hay.'

'Can't you read?' Steven asked in exasperation. 'The notices say keep out.'

'Can't read,' Mac said. 'Everybody tell Mac and Betty get out. It's winter, mister. Cold. Mac and Betty sleep in hay. Nice and warm in hay.'

Betty grinned. It was a widemouthed grimace that added nothing to her personal attractions.

'Nice and warm in hay. Nice and warm in hay. Betty cold. You got old clothes, mister, nice warm clothes you don't want for Mac and Betty?'

'You'd better get out of here, at once,' Sarah said.

'Wait a moment.' Steven could not take his eyes off Mac's boots. They were thick, strong, almost new boots, long in the leg, made to last and withstand the wet, and with sharp ridged soles that had left marks across the yard.

'Where did you get those boots?' Steven asked.

'Mac didn't steal 'em mister. Mac found 'em. Just thrown down, they was. Mac found 'em. Mac doesn't steal.'

Steven began to feel that he was trying to communicate through a fog of stupidity.

'Where did you find them?' he asked patiently. Sarah was looking at them now, and she did not want to hear the answer. She knew what it would be.

'On the farm. On the other farm. Where the funny men were.'

He looked at Betty and began to giggle. He pointed a finger at her.

'Bang Bang. Drop dead,' he shouted, and Betty began to

caper and grin. Steven experienced a sudden desire to take the two of them and throttle them.

'What funny men?' Sarah asked. They had to know now, had to know the worst, and she had met the pair before. They were well known and thoroughly unwelcome on all the farms in five counties. As a result of constant chivying they had become cunning and would steal across the fields in the dawn or dusk and hide in the hay and then make off, often with a chicken or duck neatly killed and hidden among their filthy clothing.

'Funny men in funny clothes. Silly men. Killing all the sheep. Bang. Bang. Drop dead.' Mac aimed his finger at Betty again.

Steven felt as if he had suddenly plunged twelve stories down in a fast lift.

'The farm over there?' He pointed towards Jack Dodd's sheep farm.

Mac nodded vigorously, his head jumping up and down on his neck like a disarticulated clown head.

'Bang. Bang. Drop dead. Sheep all dead. And then men burn sheep. Funny men,' he said. 'Nice and warm. Only men chase us.'

'Got away,' Betty said. 'Ran and hid in barn. Bang. Bang. Drop dead. You going to dead all your sheep, mister?'

'I'll ring the police,' Sarah said. 'They mustn't go to any more farms.' She had kept her voice low, but now she raised it. 'I'll get you some tea. Wait there, by the gate. Then you must go.'

'Nice tea,' Betty said. She began to nod too, and her tiny pink rimmed blue eyes screwed up in concentration. 'You got some nice little pigs, mister. Betty likes pigs. Betty stroked pigs.'

The lift descended again, this time even lower. Steven began to feel ill.

'Where were the boots, Mac?' he asked gently, wondering that he had enough self control left in him not to shout or scream or run for his gun and shoot this misshapen monstrous travesty of humanity as dead as Jack Dodd's sheep.

'Down by tractor. Tractor they drag sheep with. Bang,

bang. Drop dead. Funny men's clothes there too, mister. They going to kill men, mister? Saw a car crash once, Mac did. Everybody dead. Lots of blood. Lots of blood, eh Betty?'

'Betty don't like blood. Bang bang, drop dead.'

Steven wondered where Joey was, and hoped he wouldn't intrude on this insane conversation. His temper was more unpredictable than ever and he was also frequently more than half drunk, though heaven knew where the drink came from. Not even Sarah knew now. The stores she had hidden were intact, but it came from somewhere. She wondered if he was sneaking off the farm at night to go to the Goose, but not even he would dare.

Sarah came back with the tea and with large hunks of bread and jam. That would keep them quiet. Steven walked over to the pig styes. Mac's footsteps, marked out plainly in mud on the dry cobble stones, ran alongside each pen. He set his lips.

'They're on their way,' Sarah said. 'They've been hunting for them ever since they got away. The boots were left with a pile of contaminated clothing to be disinfected when the men came back from their tea break. Mac slipped in and took them while they were out. Those boots have been right into the middle of everything.'

'We could perhaps kill off the pigs,' Steven forlornly.

'How did they come on to our land?' Sarah asked.

Steven looked at her, and then went back to the couple by the gate. Their eating and drinking habits made those of his pigs pleasant by comparison. His stomach heaved when he looked at them.

'Which way did you come?' he asked.

'Mac and Betty clever,' the man said.

'How clever?' Sarah asked.

'Hide with cows. Come through sheep field. Come down at milking time. Hide in hay. Nice and warm in hay.' Mac grinned and gibbered, and Steven wished that a humane world was less humane and exposed its idiots on bleak hillsides at birth. They had more sense about animals. They killed the weaklings. He wondered absurdly if there could

85

ever be a really half-witted cow. He had certainly never met one.

He was more than thankful when the police car drove up and the sergeant got out. The constable persuaded the pair, with difficulty, that they wanted a nice ride, and the sergeant looked at Steven and shook his head.

'I'm sorry, Mr. Fenn,' he said. 'You'll have to be kept under observation. I'll tell the Vet who was over at Dodds' farm yesterday. They're disinfecting now. He'll be over some time today, and all those beasts will have to be inspected daily.'

It was all that they could hope for. Steven watched the car drive away, his thoughts bitter, and then went into the farmhouse. Sarah made coffee and passed him a pasty, but he could not eat. To distract him she turned on the wireless, but there was no solace there.

'Foot and mouth cases yesterday were fewer than on any day since the epidemic began,' a dispassionate voice announced. 'It is thought that the disease is on the wane. Which must be very good news for all farmers,' the announcer ended brightly.

Sarah slammed the kettle on to the Aga and Steven went outside, but there seemed little point in the day's chores. His farm was already under sentence of death.

CHAPTER NINE

By the next morning everybody knew that Steven's farm was under supervision. Mark and Susan Tilley telephoned to offer sympathy.

'You may be O.K. in spite of everything,' Mark said, but after a long sleepless night Steven refused to be comforted. He had had a black hour with Joey who was ready to assail the police station and lynch the two tramps, and a blacker evening when Sarah had come to say that Joey was too drunk to cope, and they had milked together in a silence that was painful, wondering if tomorrow, or the day after, the signs would show, and the parlour be empty.

Herbert Green, the landlord of the Goose, rang through before lunch.

'I'll send your next two crates of beer free,' he said. 'It's tough luck, but it might not be the end of it all, Steve.'

It was some moments before the significance of the word 'next' dawned on him.

'I've lost count of what we've had already,' he said at last, not wanting to reveal his ignorance.

'Not to worry. I'll look it up sometime. No hurry for the money. Two or three lots, that's all.'

Herbert rang off, and Steven knew at last how Joey had gained his supplies. He told Sarah.

'Herbert must have left them on the stand for the churns, along with the groceries and other things,' Sarah said. 'Joey always collects them for me. Sly old devil, I'll give him a piece of my mind.'

'It's not worth it, Sarah,' Steven said wearily. 'Leave him. We'll get over this in time, and then he'll be himself again.'

Sarah sniffed.

The Ministry Vet arrived just after lunch and accepted a cup of coffee, which he drank standing in the yard, watching the team of men look at every beast, checking feet and checking mouths, looking at eyes. Steven wondered desolately if the men might not have the infection on them, engrained in their nails or the folds of their skin, or in their hair. He did not want to see them touch his cattle, but the beasts must already be contaminated.

'How long before we know the worst?' he asked wearily. It might be better to have the disease strike and have done with it, have done with the misery of looking at each cow, wondering, of fearing the sound of a cough, or seeing lacklustre eyes or an animal that refused to eat. You could not live with fear for ever. At some stage it turned to numbness. Perhaps even the end of the suspense and the death of every animal left only numbness too, something that could not be understood, and the shock would come later. He did not know. He did not want to know. He wanted to go to bed and sleep, knowing he was safe and that the past weeks were a bad dream and this day a nightmare. He would wake. But he did not wake. The men had finished with the cows and gone to the sheep. He went out to them. They would need his dogs. The Vet walked beside him. He was so tired that he seemed to be walking in a trance. Day and night he was on call. Day and night he watched the slaughter, sick beasts and well, but mostly those that were well, as yet untouched by the contamination that caused their fellows to sicken. He had never known anything like it in the years since he qualified, and he hoped he never would again. And he had no words to comfort those that hated him, feeling that he shared the official view. He sighed deeply, and tamped tobacco into his pipe, and watched the men move through the fields.

There were only the pigs to look at now.

'How long?' Steven asked. 'Before we know the worst?'

The Vet shrugged.

'Two days, three, at the most six in this epidemic,' he said. They drove away. Another day clear.

Joey helped with the milking that night, and gave Shala

88

her bread. He stood looking at her for a long time, until she became puzzled and uneasy, and he vented a deep sigh and patted her shoulder and turned away.

'It's not right,' he said to Steven.

Steven nodded. He had now developed a cold and felt that life could not get much worse. He was tired of being cooped up, tired of Joey and his drinking, tired of Sarah and her limited interests. He wished he could open the gate and walk down the lane and call in at the Goose, and talk to Mark and the Vicar, and listen to the Master and the Huntsman arguing over the points of a good beagle, and go out and chase hares. Their own hare would not run again. Joey had seen to that, as well as ending the life of the stag and a fox that prowled unwisely. All of them were suspect carriers.

Steven went indoors but could not rest, and went outside again. Dusk was beckoning to dark, and the sombre trees moved eerily against the sky. He looked towards the sheep-field. The sheep were running downwind, bleating. All his own dogs were shut in. He took the gun and went up the hill.

A small brown dog was running among the sheep. He was not chasing them in earnest, but amusing himself. It entertained him to see the silly beasts bleating in front of him. It was much more fun than most of the games he played. He passed Steven; a raggle taggle tough little beast without a collar. No one to tell to keep him at home and indoors, no one to ask to retrieve him. Steven lifted the gun. The dog could not be allowed to run over any other farm-land. He swore violently as the little beast turned astounded eyes towards him, and died. He went back and sent Joey to bury the body in quicklime in the sour patch in the field and then telephoned the police to tell them what he had done.

'Couldn't do anything else,' the sergeant said. 'People ought to have more sense. We've got your two beauties locked up in quarantine for three weeks. Pity we can't lock them up for ever. They're a pest, always have been.'

There was another night to get through. The television set offered distraction, but he turned from a pop group to a badly made and very ancient film, and then in despair to a play that was so advanced that he could make no sense of it at all. Radio offered a choice of record programmes. He picked up a stick and went out into the night.

The moon shone over the fields. Shone on the sheep and the white patches on the bullocks' backs, shone on the heifers, and shone on the farm building. He walked up the hill and looked down at the stone building, huddled among trees. It looked warm and snug and inviting, a symbol of prosperity, of content. The milking cattle were safe in the stalls. Mick moved restlessly and struck a shoe against the stable door, the jenny donkey brayed, and her foal's small whinny answered her.

An owl hooted and flew low, a shadow against the darker sky. Frost hardened the ground and ice crystals glistened on branch and twig, on the dead thistles against the hedge, and the berries left by the birds. The brook was a shimmering ribbon of newly formed ice.

He went to the lambing shed. None of the ewes were due yet. The first, he reckoned, should give birth in about five days' time, but as he crossed the yard he was startled by the bleat of a newborn lamb and ran in, to see a small black and white body struggle to its feet, and the ewe bend her head to finish cleaning it. The first lamb of the year. It bleated again, and found food and sucked, the small tail hysterical as it wagged and the lamb tasted its first milk. It was a fine strong little beast, and would one day be a fine strong ram.

He made himself coffee and sat watching over the ewes, wide awake, in spite of the late hour. Sleep was impossible. His mind was searching for distraction. He picked up one of the books on sheep breeding that he had left on a shelf to while away long nights on watch, but there was no sense to the words, and he put it back, toyed with a copy of a farming newspaper, and then turned sharply as another of the ewes bleated. Something in the air was bringing the lambs early. He went to her, but she had no need of help and soon a second small creature was feeding happily while its mother looked at it with devotion.

It was reassuring to lie at last on the bed on the gallery above and look down on the ewes, and watch the lambs try out their steps and look about them in puzzlement, up at their mothers, at the other sheep, at the straw on the floor and the wood of their pens, at the man who watched them. He wondered what it felt like to be a newborn lamb, to have no knowledge, no means of ever finding out why the world had so many strange objects in it. How did a horse see men, he wondered, light-headed with lack of sleep, and with the streaming cold that now seemed to be an integral part of him, an added misery to those which already beset him.

And what was life like for a cow? It was an insane and profitless speculation, and at last he fell asleep, not meaning to sleep, afraid that other sheep would lamb in the night and need his help. He slept dreamlessly, heavily, and woke to hear the cattle coming for milking and Sarah's voice calling him anxiously. He jumped up guiltily. She must have been worried sick when she found he had not been in the whole night. He called her to come and see the lambs.

'Lord, you terrified me,' she said. 'I never thought of looking here. Didn't think they were due yet.'

'Neither did I,' Steven said. 'Not for at least another week, and that would have been early. But they're healthy little beasts.'

'And you might as well bloody shoot 'em,' Joey said. He came in and looked at them sourly. 'Bloody shoot the lot of them. Bloody waste of time. Bloody get a gun and shoot my bloody self.'

'Joey!' Sarah said.

He looked at her, the twinkle gone from his eyes, his mouth set, a white tightness round his lips. He swallowed.

'Bloody sow's got bloody foot-and-mouth,' he said, and went out slamming the door, and left Steven looking at his two new lambs, and Sarah with a face whiter than a sheep's fleece, gripping one of the pens for support.

CHAPTER TEN

NIGHTMARE became reality, and reality, nightmare. Steven went to look at the sow, hoping that Joey might be wrong, but there was no mistake. Weakened by birth only a few days before, Batty Betty had infected her when she stroked her and she was already very sick. She lay staring up at him, and he looked down at her, knowing that with her illness came the death sentence on all his beasts.

He spoke on the telephone to the police sergeant, who needed no one to tell him that this conversation was better cut short.

'Too bloody bad,' he said, meaning it most sincerely. 'I'll cope.'

Steven was grateful for his brevity. He went into the morning. The catttle were calling and needed milking. It was absurd to milk them, and the milk would have to be thrown away, but he could not leave them all day in discomfort. He called the dog and rounded them into the yard and Sarah came. It was worse than any death ceremony, washing them down, fastening the cups, listening to the clatter of the machine, watching the gallons pour out, knowing that the cows would be dead by nightfall, knowing that the beast that was so warm under your hand would be rigid, with staring eyes and legs pointing to the sky and then would end as a heap of ashes. It was also impossible to realize. It was a cessation of sanity.

The police guard for the gates arrived with the Vet. The men had nothing to say. They had been there before, and pity was blunted by use. The Vet looked at the sow. He said nothing for a long time. His temper had vanished days ago, he was tired, he was angry, he was sick of the futility and the waste, yet he knew there was no alternative. He wanted to wave a magic wand, to say 'Beast, be well,' to ease the pain that he was seeing daily. At least here there were no children to cry. Sarah might weep, but her tears would never be on view. He had seen her finishing the milking and walk slowly, as if her legs belonged to somebody else, towards the farmhouse.

'It's foot and mouth all right, Steve,' the Vet said. He pushed his hair wearily out of his eyes. He was sure it must be grey by now, and that he had aged by over a century since the epidemic began. No peace for the wicked, and that was as bloody silly a phrase as any that his tired brain could dredge up. He went to telephone.

'There were two lambs born in the night,' Steven said and then wished he had not spoken. His mind had been full of his own plight, and the face that the Vet turned to him suddenly revealed the whole travesty of horror that the man had seen in the past weeks.

'Here, you need a drink.'

'I'll go out like a light if I have one,' the Vet said, 'but can Sarah rustle me some food? I didn't get home last night. There was another case over the other side of the county, and two of our team are down with flu. I'd just got in when I got the message about your farm.'

Sarah was thankful to have something to do. She made quantities of tea and bacon and eggs and took sandwiches out to the policemen and then went to find Joey, but he had vanished. Steven made only a pretence at eating. He drank two cups of tea, and Sarah, hearing him sneeze and sneeze again, brought him two aspirins for his cold. As he took them he thought how easy it would be to empty the bottle, and end the horror that had overtaken him with day.

The slaughterers arrived. He could not bear to look at them, feeling them tainted, horrible creatures, on a par with mediaeval executioners. He heard them joking outside and looked up at the Vet, sickened.

'They'd go mad if they didn't make light of it, Steve,' he said. 'It's like doctors and nurses, joking round a death

93

bed. You can only stand so much. You have to have a shell. Otherwise you'd break up.'

He sat down and stretched out his legs and Black Cat, after thoughtfully inspecting his boot, brought him one of her kittens, which she still carried about, although it was far too big for such an undignified mode of treatment, and it protested vocally in a small plaintive tone that made the men smile at one another, glad to have their mood lightened.

The Vet stretched his legs out further, picked up the little beast, and sighed.

'A short break and then to work. I'll never get used to all this slaughter,' he added, almost to himself. 'Hundreds of thousands of healthy beasts all sacrificed. I know it's necessary, I know that at present there isn't any decent cure and the disease goes through every beast in the herd, every sheep in the flock, every pig in the stye. Afterwards the beasts may be barren, their feet overgrow, and they're lame. they're more prone to disease. But I keep thinking that while we have a slaughter policy we don't have research, that if we had more experimental work we might find a cure, find a preventative, find an all-purpose vaccine that could be injected into a beast at birth and protect it against everything. We found a method for brucellosis, we can fight any number of other horrible things, but this one . . . we give up. We kill, because it's cheaper to compensate than to inoculate, because inoculation isn't good enough yet, because we don't want to have a barrier of immune beasts round an infected zone in case they aren't immune, in case they become carriers, in case we never get rid of the disease. It's all so bloody sensible, the things we do for expediency, and it's all so bloody wicked.'

'If every farmer paid ten pounds a year to a central fund for research maybe we could sponsor something, or set up a proper team to find out how the thing spreads, and how it can be kept out,' Steven said. 'Mine is easy . . . those two maniacs brought it here – but how did it get to Jack, right out of the blue, some days after everyone thought the area was safe again? How did it start in the first place? And mightn't it be here all the time, not among cattle at all, but

94

among deer? Deer are breeding all over the country, I've had one here for some years, an old fellow who came to steal our hay, and there must be others. They get it too, and who's to say that it didn't get to them on the wind, or brought by people picnicking in the woods, and then spread to outlying farms, and then spread again?'

'Nobody knows,' the Vet said wearily.

He went. Steven was left alone in the farmhouse. They were killing his cattle. He thought bitterly of Idiot Mac. Bang. Bang. You're dead. The men were talking and laughing, one of them was even singing, and the beasts were lowing. The cats were shut in and the noise and bustle had alarmed Tom Cat so much that he had gone to ground under an old oak chest on the landing, and nothing could be seen of him but two wide green eyes, as he glared out at a world that had suddenly gone mad.

Bob and Bess were both upset. Bess was soon to pup, perhaps that day, and was restless. Normally she dug herself a tunnel, but she could not get out, and she tried to dig in a pile of newspaper. Sarah gave her a box and lined that with paper, and Bess teased it into small strips until the kittens saw her and came to join the game and smothered the floor with torn and chewed pulp. Bob looked out of the window and saw one of the men in the field lift the humane killer, and saw the cow fall, and suddenly raised his voice in a long eerie howl that went on and on, driving Sarah and Steven almost witless, as time and again he added to the din.

There was nowhere to go and nothing to do. Steven saw a man lead Shala out of the stall and across the yard. She turned a gently inquiring head, expecting friends and expecting bread, and finding neither, lowed forlornly. Sarah gave a strangled gasp and fled round the back of the farmhouse into the jenny donkey's stable, where she could be alone and uninterrupted, and Steven was sick, reaching the downstairs bathroom just in time, retching uselessly and endlessly, unable to control himself. He came to the kitchen and collapsed into the armchair, unaware that one of the policemen had come inside to look for him, and hearing him, had made a pot of tea, and stayed to see if he could help. Steven took the tea, scarcely aware of his surroundings.

If only the day would go and the end of it come and all the beasts dead. Instead he was aware of them as if he had been watching. Aware of the sheep on the hill and the bullocks in the field and the heifers beyond them. And the cattle in the stalls. Only there were no cattle in the stalls. Shala had been the last of them. Her calves would be unborn, her pedigree lost, no rosette would ever proclaim her Best in Show or Champion Milker. Nor any daughter of hers.

The sheep would be next. He could not bear to think of the new lambs, last night so eager and alive, so aware of their surroundings, their eyes bright, their small tails wagging busily, their mothers proud. It was no use. He was going to be sick again. The policeman watched him unhappily. He came from farming stock too and his parents had lost their beasts. His mother was in hospital. Shock, they said. It wasn't right.

To the noise and the bustle was added the sound of flames as the pits were stoked, and the stench of flesh came next. The black pall poured across the horizon and everyone in the village looked towards Hollow End and thought of Steven Fenn and was saddened. In her small cottage Susan Tilley cried until her eyes ached and her face was puffed and she could neither speak to Mark nor do more than make tea for the two of them and dissolve into tears again, wishing that she could comfort Steven, who had been kind to her.

Not even Mark knew how kind. Mark seemed so little aware of the need for money that he often left his wife very short. Steven, coming to visit her one day when she was struggling with her budget, helped her balance her accounts, and was shocked to find how little money she had for food. After that when he came he always brought a gift; a sack of potatoes, eggs, or a dressed chicken, green vegetables of all kinds from Sarah's kitchen garden and fruit when it was in season. Sometimes a rabbit or a hare, and once or twice a pheasant was added to her menu. She had missed his gifts in the past weeks, and also his visits, as he reminded her of her own father, who was dead, and he was easy to talk to, and Mark, with his quick tempers and extravagant moods, was far from easy to live with.

Just now Mark, too, was on edge. The Goose was dull without the farmers, and he was unhappily aware that he could not draw unless he drew from life, and he could not do that with every beast in quarantine. Also he had been using several of Steven's cows as models, and the drawings, which had taken valuable hours, would have to be scrapped. And until he could finish the work he would not get paid, and their funds were very low indeed. He was not well known and had to make a name for himself, and there was a limit to the number of people who wanted pictures of animals. And if he was late with his work, that was a black mark. He doubted if people in London would realize that he had been affected by the epidemic. It sounded so damned silly.

Susan was no help. She cried if he looked at her, a fact that was more due to being worried by lack of money than to anything else, although her sympathy for Steven was sincere. He spent more and more time out of the cottage, Mark most of it with Tyrant, schooling him until he was so well trained that he could work without a rider, and would go from one side of the field to another, jumping by himself, or would dance for Mark, while Mark whistled, and end his display by standing erect, neighing noisily.

In the Goose at night there was no one to sing to, but Mark sang, improvising as he went. He sang folk songs that he made up himself, and one night, thoroughly bored, he picked a noisy quarrel with a cattle cake representative from London, who had been trying to get information about the state of the farmers after foot and mouth. The man had eager eyes and a wet mouth and Mark disliked him on sight, and disliked him even more after a few minutes' conversation.

'We don't like strangers in the Goose,' he commented finally, and picked up his guitar and began to strum, improvising a piece of ribaldry that made the man furious.

Finally he went.

'You oughtn't to have done that,' the landlord said. 'Not that he didn't deserve it. He did.'

'People like that make me sick,' Mark said angrily. 'Gloating over other people's miseries. With those silly little pig eyes. Like the idiots that come to gawp and watch beasts being killed. People make me sick.'

It became his stock phrase. He schooled Tyrant and drew Copper, the Persian cat. Susan began to write about the cat, and Mark illustrated her story. Perhaps they could sell it and perhaps the publishers would pay early and perhaps they could eat properly again. Mark had been unable to go to any farm and draw his beasts for over ten weeks. And what was worse, he had no money for feed for Tyrant.

'I'll have to sell him,' he said to Susan.

'It would be like selling one of us,' Susan said, and that was that. The afternoon that the slaughterers came to Hollow End she drew out the last of her savings from the post office, and went to the village shop to ask them to buy feed for the horse. None of the local farms could even give them hay. And the grass in the field where he lived was very poor and what was more, the shed wasn't adequate shelter. They *would* have to sell him, she thought glumly, and then looked across the fields and saw the pyre burning and ran indoors again.

'Oh, God,' Mark said, and saddled the horse, and walked him down the lanes.

CHAPTER ELEVEN

STEVEN had lost track of the days, and not until he saw
the cars coming towards the farm did he realize it was Satur-
day. Surely to heaven people would not come down the lane.
But the cars parked and the inquisitive clambered out, and
walked along the verges and down the middle of the road,
jabbering excitedly, pointing at the disinfectant cans, and at
the policemen, at the straw mats and the notices, at the men
in the field, visible over the hedge and up the hill, engaged in
slaughtering the sheep.

The police were busy. Cars blocked the end of the lane
and had to be moved. The over-inquisitive had to be kept
away from the gates, from standing on the banks to try and
see the slaughterers, from parking anywhere and everywhere,
anxious only not to miss a moment of this unusual excitement.

Joey surfaced briefly. He had hidden his crates under the
hay in the loft where Sarah bred rabbits. No one would
think of looking up there. He felt a momentary twinge of
guilt, knowing perfectly well that he should not have ordered
the beer, or used Steven's name. Too late now to care. The
reckoning would come when Herbert sent the bill. He un-
earthed another bottle, and then heard voices outside in the
lane.

He looked out of the tiny loft window, a mere hole cut
in the wood, and stared at the people milling outside.
Surely to heaven they hadn't come to watch, to see the
beasts die? But it was soon plain that they had, that this
was strange, exciting, even exhilarating, something that
had never happened before in their dull lives and might
not happen again. As more beasts were added to the pyre

the voices grew louder, and laughter punctuated the din.

It was cold. The sky was black with lowering cloud, and snow was beginning to fall. Yet even this did not deter the watchers beyond the gates. Children tried to catch the falling flakes, and ran and screamed with delight, and their parents turned up coat collars and stood staring as if this were some play set up for them on the television screen, with no thought whatever for the misery that lay behind the scene.

Joey began to climb down the ladder. His legs were unsteady, and he slipped, but fell softly in the hay, and stood up again, and weaved his way across the yard. Nobody saw him. Steven was lying on his bed, fighting off the sickness that had attacked him, and Sarah could not have come out of the jenny donkey's stable to save her life. Her ears were assaulted with the noise of the men and the milling beasts, now fewer and fewer each hour, and Bob howled uncannily, sure that his world had disintegrated about him.

Joey walked into the kitchen. The gun was leaning against the wall. He loaded it with trembling hands. Beer and anger were multiplying inside him, mounting to gigantic proportions. He went into the yard, and began to walk towards the gate. People close to the hedge saw the gun muzzle lift and aim straight at their faces.

'All right, you silly sods,' Joey yelled. Steven heard him, and pulled himself wearily up off the bed, and went downstairs. 'Stay there, and you'll get it. Get it in your faces. Drop dead, the lot of you, like those poor brutes out there that led a better life than you ever led, God rot you. God rot the whole bleeding stinking lot of you.'

The police sergeant was inside the gate.

'Joey, put it down, man. You can't shoot them. Come on now, give it to me.'

'Shoot the whole sodding lot.' Joey lifted the gun. Snow flaked his hair and shoulders, snow swirled out of the dulling sky, snow speckled the onlookers. Snow fell on the gun. 'Sod off, the lot of you. Get out.'

He fired wildly into the air, and one of the constables, who

100

had slipped round, unseen, and come behind him, pinioned his arms. The sergeant took the gun and unloaded it. He went to put it back in the kitchen, but changed his mind. Joey might run amok again.

Sarah had heard the shot. She came out into the yard, her face unrecognizable. Tears blurred her features and her eyes were swollen. She kept her head resolutely away from the fields behind her. It was one thing to breed beasts for market. It was another to be present at their death. She was not sure that she could ever eat mutton again, or beef for that matter. She went over to Joey.

'Come on,' she said. 'Bed for you, my man. Bed, Joey, come on.'

Joey blinked at her. He looked at the sheep field. The packed backs were fewer but there were still living beasts there. As he watched, one of them, panic-stricken, leaped the backs of several others and made a headlong dash for safety. One of the men cut her off, the humane killer did its swift work, and she was dead. Joey looked at the people who had come back to the gate in spite of the police sergeant asking them to move away.

'Dilly dilly, dilly dilly,
Come and be killed.

For we must sell our sheep and the fools must be filled,' he shouted the words in a singsong, over and over again as Sarah led him inside. The watchers at the gate were uneasy, but they were not going to miss any of the fun. They were all strangers. None of the actors in this drama was known to them. They crowded close, expectantly.

Mark, riding Tyrant down the lanes, saw their heads, and stared, and swore. He put the horse to a gate and sped across fields towards the farm, landing in the lane with a clatter of hooves that made the crowd turn to survey this newcomer to their scene.

Mark saw Sarah leading Joey indoors. Joey was staggering and shouting, and Sarah walked as if she was an automaton. Steven was standing in the doorway, unable to think of anything to do or to say. All will power seemed to have left him. Events had suddenly been taken out of his hands.

101

He felt as if he were at the wheel of a car that had lost all its controls, plunging downwards to disaster, unable to stop himself. Mark, looking at him, was angry. Angry at the senseless way in which Fate singled out her victims. What had poor old Steve done to deserve this?

'Cor, it makes yer think,' a man standing beyond him said. Mark doubted the statement. He wanted to disperse the crowd, to leave Steven in peace, to clear the lane, and he did not know how to start. The snow, now beginning to lie, did not deter anyone. These were the people who spent days and nights on end watching one disaster or another, feeding on misery as a sparrow fed on fat, finding it a rare and delightful treat.

'Ghouls. Vampires,' Mark said furiously.

'They come to all the killings. You see the same faces over and over again,' the sergeant said. He frowned unhappily. 'I wish I could get rid of them. We keep moving them back but it's not easy, and I don't want anyone to slip through for a closer look, and some of them are quite capable of it.'

One of the children, running down the lane, trying to flick at another boy with a switch made from a willow twig, slashed Tyrant on the hock. Mark had been watching Steven, wishing he could go inside and talk to him, distract him, anything to take away the look on his face. But if he did he would have to go into quarantine. Poor old Steve. He was almost unseated when Tyrant reared and whinnied in shrill indignation. He regained control and brought the horse on to the road again, losing his temper completely. The people close to him moved back.

'Dangerous brute,' a woman said.

Mark, never conventional, needed no other goad. He turned and cantered up the road, and the people watched him go, and sighed with relief, and turned to the killing again. They were startled when Mark came back at a gallop, yelling 'Charge' at the top of his voice. They began to run.

When he was level with the gate he reined Tyrant to a standstill, a circus standstill, a showy horse standing on hind-

102

legs, with beating hooves and shrill neigh, towering above them.

Mark's voice rang out in the now silent lane.

'I'll sing you a song O.'

Faces were turned towards him, to this big bearded extravagantly dressed man astride his gleaming chestnut horse. This was an unlooked for entertainment. Mark's voice rang out above the noises, every word clear.

> 'What is your song O?
> I'll sing you a song of an idiot race
> Who came to stand in the market place
> To stand and stare at the farmer's fears
> As the pride of his heart and the work of years
> Was brutally killed and reduced to dust.
> They came to gloat and indulge their lust.
> That is my song O.'

People were looking at one another, and then not looking at one another. Uneasy, disliking this sudden assault upon them, afraid of a man who could be so unconventional, and of the horse that was now prancing in a small circling dance, they walked towards their cars. Mark had not finished with them yet.

He galloped down the lane, releasing anger in movement. At the end he turned and galloped back, yelling above the sound of hooves.

> 'I'll sing you a song of a man so coarse
> That he tramped the filthy mob with his horse . . .

and he sped towards them just as Sarah came to the end of her tether too, and turned the hose on full blast and directed it over the hedge. The retreat became a riot as people pelted out of reach of the galloping horse and of the torrent of water. Children screamed, and their parents ran, and then stood out of range, shouting with fury.

A police inspector, climbing out of his car at the end of the lane, looked at the scene.

'It's an outrage,' one man said, shaking his fist at the farm.

'An outrage?' The inspector asked. 'Were you invited in the first place?'

He turned and walked down the lane, and then began to direct cars out on to the main road. Mark patrolled on his horse. He hurried the slow by forcing Tyrant to rear, and no one stopped to argue.

Steven waved to him, too tired to speak. Mark went home to Susan at the end of the day, weary and anxious, and found Susan almost distraught.

CHAPTER TWELVE

ROBBIE had spent the week brooding. He belonged, more than anywhere, to Salem Hardacre. He spent much of his time in the Goose and knew the men. He had been ordered to interview Ed Lucas for his paper, but Ed had been tired and surly, and had either not answered his questions or had sworn at him. Robbie did not blame him. He wondered if he ought to invent something, but that wasn't his way, so he wrote nothing, and that night arrived home so drunk that his landlady threw him out in the morning.

Herbert Green gave him a room. Robbie was old, and ill, and tired, and Herbert knew how he felt. It was too much effort to get up early and go out, too much effort to take any heed at all of his editor's telephoned instructions, and he didn't want to interview the farmers. If the women's page wanted Mollie Martin to tell them how she felt, waiting, wondering, then they could send someone else. He knew how Mollie felt. He knew the years of work that had gone into making that Jersey herd, knew that Mollie was too soft for a farmer's wife, fond of all her beasts, finding in them a pleasure that was out of all proportion to their value and had nothing whatever to do with the wealth that the herd brought the farm.

He knew how Steven would feel. He knew, better than anyone, of the immense satisfaction that Steven had derived from his change of occupation. Robbie would have liked to farm. He had always had a way with animals. Cats adored him, and dogs followed him, and he could handle Ed's birds with perfect confidence, a telling test, as birds of prey were tricky, unpredictable creatures.

He was not going to see Steven, nor the farm, nor the

beasts that lay on the pyres. Mac could go and take photographs, if he chose. Robbie was going to sit in the Goose and drink a little and dream a little. He had had flu, and was left with a horrible depression. Dream of what he would say to his editor, and how he would give notice. Nobody would suffer but himself. And he was almost old enough to retire. He wondered how it would be to be free of the need to earn money, to have enough to drink the rest of his life away. But the Goose was too near to Hollow End. He could see the fires and hear the noise, and at last he went out into the snow and went to see Susan.

Sue was sitting in front of the fire holding the cat, who disliked being handled. When he saw Robbie he gave a delighted mew, and deserted his mistress.

'Beastly animal,' she said.

Robbie lifted the cat into his arms and sat down on the sofa. He wanted to sit and think, to be alone, yet he needed company.

'Haven't any conversation, today,' he said. He grinned, wryly.

'I can only think of Steve,' Sue said forlornly. 'I'll make some tea.'

'It's a rotten world,' Robbie said. 'Plays dirty rotten tricks on people. Never on the right people. Thugs, thieves, killers, they get away with everything. Get away with murder.' He laughed, but without amusement. 'And some innocent who's never done a day's harm in his life, gets punished by something the Church calls divine wrath. Plague over England. Did you ever wonder what it was really like, Sue?'

'Yes,' Susan said. 'I had to when I was writing about it. I think I managed to terrify myself completely. I'll never be able to go back and look at the old village.'

'I heard the bull last night at Hollow End,' Robbie said. 'Went walking in the lane, and heard the bull.'

'You heard owls,' Susan said. She did not like the lane at night. It was spooky and leaves brushed against those who walked near the hedge, and there were screech owls in the hollow oak, and the noisy cattle breathing in unison, a vast deep sigh in the dark. She did not want to believe in ghosts as well. Living horrors could be bad enough.

'They say that anyone who hears the bull is going to die,' Robbie said. 'I think it must be nice to be dead. Peaceful. No one badgering or bothering you. No need to eat or drink or get up in the morning. No hunger, no cold. Nobody to hurt you.'

'And no sun, no moon, and no tomorrow. I couldn't bear to be dead, Robbie, and not know what was happening to those around me.'

'You're young,' Robbie said. 'If you ever have a son, Sue, call him Robbie for me. Will you?'

'You can be godfather,' Susan said. She was beginning to worry. Robbie was often mournful, but he had never talked like this before.

'It was Mary Queen of Scots who wrote, "Only the dead are beautiful and free,"' Robbie went on, as if he had not even heard her. 'Do you know the tower in the old village, Sue? Bat-haunted, and overgrown with ivy, with birds nesting in the creepers and owls calling. Those owls must be the source of the old stories. Owls and jays screaming day and night. And the souls of the dead. I wonder if beasts have souls? If so there must be a good many struggling for existence somewhere else.'

'Robbie, you're ill,' Susan said.

'I'm not ill, love. I'm well. And I'm stone cold sober for a change. Perhaps that was a mistake. It doesn't do to look at the world out of sober eyes. You see what's wrong, and you feel sure that men can never put it right.'

'One day they will,' Susan said.

'This year, next year, sometime, never. Robbie's too old and tired to hope, my love.'

He leaned towards her and put the cat in her arms.

'Look after Copper for me and don't forget your promise,' he said. He looked down at her. His blue eyes were tired. He bent and kissed her on the forehead. 'Good-bye, little Sue.'

He went out, slowly, his feet dragging, and Sue called after him, but he did not look back. He turned the corner and was

107

gone. She had never been so relieved in all her life as she was when Mark came home.

Mark listened to her, and said nothing.

He walked to the window and lifted the curtain. Down the village street and up the hill was the old village. The hill matched that on which Steven ran his sheep. Twilight was drawing to dusk. Mark went to the telephone, as uneasy as Susan had been.

The Vicar listened.

'Meet me outside the vicarage gate,' he said.

It was cold. Snow masked the ground and deadened their footsteps. At the other end of the village the flames were dying. The Vicar, looking back, thought of ancient sacrifices to unknown gods, and shivered. He, too, was feeling his age.

A hooting owl savaged the stillness. There had never been such a night in the village. Not a living beast walked on the nearby farms; no sound of cow, or moving sheep, or grunting pig. The lifting moon shone on fields that were deserts, bleak and empty, and on the hill above them, where stark ruins stood wicked black against the skyline.

Nothing moved in the night. The wind was quiet, the trees motionless as in a vision. The dark branches interlaced, snow silvered the trunks, and softened the hedges and drifted gently downwards, great damp flakes that caught in eye and nostril, and seeped down scarves and jacket collars.

The snow beneath the trees did not hide the footsteps. Mark looked at the Vicar. There were no words to say. They followed the dark track to the foot of the old tower. The doorway gaped black. Mark did not want to go inside, nor to stay outside. Here, on the lonely hill, with nothing to mar the white but the trail across the snow, it was easy to believe that the dead walked. Easy to believe that those who had suffered and died from plague found no rest. Easy to believe that the rustle in bushes came from nothing that lived. He pulled his coat collar higher around his ears.

There was drifting snow and dust inside the tower. The Vicar shone his torch. They were not surprised to see Robbie looking down on them, his face ghastly, his eyes

108

wide, as he swung at the end of the rope tied to the rafters.

'It's too late,' the Vicar said, but they cut him down, and Mark, lying on the ground with his mouth against the dead man's mouth, trying to breathe life into the useless lungs, could only think that now another ghost would haunt the village, and that the new plague had found another victim, a victim who would never be acknowledged.

He was colder than ever. He stood up as the Vicar returned with the doctor and two policemen and a stretcher.

'It's no use,' he said.

He watched them walk down the hill. Behind him the moon shone clear and cold. An owl watched him from a tree. Its weird cry ululated from its throat, and far away, another bird answered.

'Whoo . . . whooo . . . whooo.'

The village was alive with ghosts. They ran from the houses, jumped from the ground, slid from behind trees, mocked and jeered and murmured to him, their insistent voices calling him, so that he turned and ran headlong, plunging downhill in primitive terror, running from fear, from dread, from things not understood, and from the memory of Robbie, swinging above him, looking down, acknowledging that life had defeated him and there was nothing left but death.

CHAPTER THIRTEEN

THEY had all gone and Steven was alone. Sarah had put Joey to bed, and had fallen asleep, exhausted, in an armchair in her kitchen. Outside, in the stables, Mick neighed.

Steven was startled. The horses had not been fed or watered, and the jenny donkey needed feeding too. He had forgotten that any beasts were left. The slaughterers could have killed all three and he would not have noticed.

It was an effort to fill the buckets and measure the feed, an effort to stand and empty the mixture into the mangers, an effort to ted hay into the hayracks. He moved so slowly that he felt as if he were sleepwalking. The pitchfork weighed a ton as he lifted the soiled straw to the barrow. He took the straw to the midden. He went back and tedded clean straw beneath the horses. He was too tired to groom them, and they had not been touched for two days. He would do it tomorrow.

He had never been afraid at night before, but the farm was uncanny. Nothing moved in the empty pigsties. No beasts lowed in the stalls. No sheep lay in the grass beneath the trees, or bleated in the new lambing shed. There had been no evening milking. Nothing to clean tonight, and the men had hosed the yard before they left. Tomorrow troops were coming to help disinfect the place. Disinfectant and whitewash. It would blot everything out. Blot out the vision of Shala asking Joey for bread, of Shala turning to the men who led her, her face puzzled. Surely tonight all his beasts walked again? Surely they haunted the quiet fields, unable to understand what had happened to them.

Steven shivered. His cold was worse, and he felt hot and shaky, and then shivered and could not get warm. He closed the stable door, and went inside and fed the cats and the dogs. Bess was uneasy and Bob was restless, and the sheep-dogs seemed puzzled. It was cold in their pen and he took them out and put them in the leanto against the kitchen wall where the Aga was warm. He turned off the heat in byre and stall and shed. There was no sense in wasting money. He left the immersion heater going in case the water froze and the pipes burst.

He wished that he had someone to talk to, now that he was alone. He enjoyed talking to other men, talking to Robbie, who had a wide knowledge of the world, even if he was un-usually cynical. The cynicism hid a gentleness that Robbie would never admit.

He hoped that Ken was safe. Ken's farm was close to him, but the cattle were all inside, and sometimes he could smell Mollie's onions on the wind. He was irrationally glad that he had not used borax or any other remedy for his own herd. Nothing could stand against the pure bad luck that had come to him when Idiot Mac hid in his hay stack.

If he were lucky he could re-stock in six weeks. Perhaps the epidemic would be over before then. He wondered if the virus lay in his soil, if the birds that haunted the fields could take it to Ken, if the dogs carried it on their paws.

He went into the kitchen. The fire was low, but he did not want to mend it. He sat, hands hanging loose between his legs, unable to sleep, unable to think, racked over and over again by shivering fits. He must have flu again. Another kind of virus. He lay back in the chair, and looked out at the night.

The moon shone full, hanging low in the sky, shone on the empty fields. There were stars too. Millions of miles away. Men hoped to soar to the stars. There were no beasts up there, there was no sense up there, but perhaps there was more peace up there. If there were demons and angels and ghosts, then his farm would be haunted for years to come. He could not forget Shala's anxious expression. It wasn't fair, that a man should stay conscious and think and brood at a time when the rest of the world was asleep.

The gun was in the corner again. The sergeant had leaned

it against the wall. He picked it up and looked at it as if he had never seen it before. Slowly an idea began to take shape. He would join his beasts and end his life out there in the quiet, where they had died.

He loaded the gun, looked at the dogs, and went into the night. Infinite silence where there had been noise, and an infinite peace that was senseless.

He was too old to start again. He had had a good life, but this was the end. He wished that Jenny was in the farmhouse, that he could go to her and find comfort, but she was gone, long ago. It was hard to remember her face. And the children had their own lives and would never miss him. Joey and Sarah . . . they would manage. He had left them a share in the farm in his will. No one else would want Hollow End.

Hollow End. He began to laugh. Hollow mockery that he should find fulfilment and lose it again in such a place. He had never realized before that the name had any significance. He would not be the first to come to a violent end – a hollow end. There had been the boy savaged by the bull. It was easy to imagine the bull. It was easy to imagine the peace that came with death. He raised the gun.

Mark had run down the hill, away from his own demons. He had to call in at the police station and make a statement but had asked if he could tell Susan first, so that she would not worry. He raced down the lane towards his cottage. Hollow End was dark, except for a single light spilling from the kitchen window, spilling across the yard, and glinting, dear God, on the shotgun that Steven was holding in his hand. Mark vaulted the gate and ran, his heart pounding, sickness welling into his throat.

Dear God, not again. Not again.

Steven heard nothing. He was looking at the farm, at the fields, at the buildings that had meant so much to him and that now meant nothing. Full of sound and fury, signifying nothing. They were no longer full of sound. In a minute, he would pull the trigger. He looked at the trees and the stars and the moon, and the snow that was gently falling. He was burning hot in spite of the cold. He shivered.

Mark took the gun. There was no resistance.

'Steve, you're ill. My god, man, you'll catch pneumonia sitting out here.'

Steven began to laugh. How could a dead man catch pneumonia? He let Mark lead him indoors and help him to the settee, and watched without much interest as he brought pillows and eiderdown and blankets from the bedroom, banked the fire to a blaze and put a kettle on to boil. He found the aspirins that Sarah had left in the kitchen and shook three into his hand. He gave them to Steven, who took them like a child, asking no question, suddenly no longer part of the world.

Mark went to the telephone.

Susan listened. Mark could not come for her, as he would now have to isolate himself. She must come to him. Steven needed nursing, and Sarah was probably not able to cope alone. She would come at once. Mrs. Roach, the Vicar's housekeeper, would pack for her tomorrow. Their things could be brought to the farm gate. She ran down the lane, her heart thudding as she passed the corner. Nothing stirred in the dark. And then, behind her, she heard hoofbeats. She paused, terrified, and a beast nuzzled her, and she screamed. There were no beasts. The bull was here. The ghost had come for her. A faint reproachful snuffle made her open her eyes. Tyrant had jumped the hedge and followed her. She almost fainted.

'Just as well he did,' Mark said, when he met them at the gate and she told him of her fright. 'Steve's got food here for the horses and we can put the poor old boy in a decent stable. It's cold in his field tonight. Have you got our night things?'

He took the basket from her, and began to open it.

Mark looked at her as she sat down and laughed, and went on laughing until tears came, and the basket lid was open, revealing Copper, staring up at his master haughtily. With a supreme gesture of contempt he climbed out on to the table. She had not remembered anything else.

There was a spit of fury and a flurry. Tom Cat was not tolerating another cat on his territory. Mark did not dare

113

separate the fighting beasts, but, as Copper fled, Susan grabbed him and pushed him back in the basket.

'He'll just have to stay there until we can think what to do,' she said.

Steven was asleep. She covered him gently, and began to drink the tea that Mark had brought her, while Mark himself telephoned the police station and was told to stay where he was and not, on any account, to leave Steven Fenn on his own.

He spoke to the doctor next. Isolation or not, Steven needed medicine. Mark passed the time making up fresh buckets of disinfectant. He did not want to go to sleep, although he had hidden the gun and also the ammunition.

Susan watched the darkness turn grey, and yawned. It was a long night.

A cold nose touched her fingers. She looked down. Bess had crept to her, a beseeching expression in her brown eyes. One pup dangled from her, half born. Mark came to the rescue and eased the tiny beast into the world. Susan knelt on the rug, holding the bitch's head, and one by one, nine puppies wriggled into the room, and lay whimpering.

Susan put them in a box, on an old piece of blanket, wrapped round a hot water bottle. She put Bess with them, after helping the bitch clean herself, but Bess would have none of them. She climbed on to the settee and lay with her nose on her master's arm, curled up against his body. Finally, sure that the pups ought to be fed, Susan put them with the bitch, hoping that none of them would fall to the floor.

Bess began to lick them, and let them suckle, but her eyes never left Steven's face.

Outside in the yard a cock crowed to welcome day; a day that had piled snow outside and that signalled more to come. Susan had forgotten the chickens. She wondered if Sarah was awake. She did not have to wonder long. Sarah had been worried about her employer, and woke, as always, at milking time. Although no cows needed her, she dressed and went across the kitchen, where she was astonished to see Mark and Susan.

114

'Just as well you were passing,' she said, when she heard Mark's story of the night before.

He went out to see to the horses while Sarah sent Susan off to sleep for a while, as the girl was too tired to eat. He tedded hay for Mick and Grey and Tyrant, and thought how odd it was that if Robbie hadn't died up there in the night, he would never have passed the farmhouse, or seen Steven.

Tyrant nosed him eagerly, greedy for food.

'Poor old lad, we've all been on short commons,' Mark said.

The doctor's car drew up in the lane and Mark went to meet him, ware of the silence in the once noisy farm and the smoother of snow and the icy morning.

CHAPTER FOURTEEN

Two days later, Steven's despair seemed almost a dream. The numbness of shock was wearing away, and he was able to look about him again and take an interest in events round him. Bess refused to leave him, and her squirming pups, lying on newspaper on a blanket beside him, were not only entertainment, but a promise. New life had already come to the farm. In a few weeks there would be cattle in the sheds again. Six weeks, eight weeks ... the epidemic was on the wane, possibly his was the last case. The precautions taken, the fight to stop the spread to further counties, at last showed results.

Sarah was making plans too. The men outside, noisy and boisterous, were scrubbing and disinfecting, burying the huge midden in a pit dug out in one of the fields, laughing and joking. When they had gone she intended her own campaign. There would never be such a springcleaning. They would whitewash everywhere inside the farmhouse and cottage, wash curtains, covers, blankets, and polish every piece of furniture. With no cattle to milk, or pigs to feed, or lambs to watch over, there was all the time in the world, and she was not going to waste it.

The lambing shed would make a drying shed where heavy articles could be hung. She would clean out the pantry and Joey could mend everything that needed mending. They would tidy the fences and hedges and concrete the patch down by the brook where muddy water overflowed every year.

Tom Cat and Black Cat were banished to an empty cattle stall with the kittens, as neither would tolerate Copper, who already had a torn ear and a scratched nose, although Tom

Cat had a bite on his leg and Black Cat had several scratches to prove Copper was no coward. The cats preferred the outside world. Soon they could roam freely again, and so could the dogs, who were bored and irritable, shut in the run all day. Mark took them, one at a time, into the biggest barn for a romp with stick and ball, so that every time he passed them they barked and whined for him to exercise them again.

Joey mucked out the stables, and came in for his coffee and stood on one leg, with his foot behind him, looking at Steven like a schoolboy expecting blame.

'Cheer up, Joey,' Steven said, though far from cheerful himself.

'I wasn't much help,' Joey said, not able to find words, wanting to apologize and not knowing how.

'Takes people different ways,' Steven said. He felt as if he had been ill for weeks, and the episode with the gun had faded into unreality. How could he have been such a fool? Thank God Mark had seen him. He had never been a man for despair and now found it hard to understand what could have prompted him.

'Post flu depression,' the doctor had said. 'And shock.' He sighed.

Sarah, who had been watching him like a mother hen, brought a fountain pen filler full of milk and lifted one of the pups.

'You can make yourself useful, Mr. Fenn,' she said firmly. 'Bess can't rear that lot alone so we're all going to have to help her. I've got homes for all nine pups, so we're not losing a single one.'

Susan was kept busy too. None of them were going to have time to brood. Work cured everything, in Sarah's opinion, and she had spent all her sorrow two days before on the jenny donkey's furry neck, standing, desolate, in the dark stables, hearing the beasts she had tended die, one by one. It had been a never-ending day. So many of them, and worst of all the two new lambs. Sarah loved lambing time.

She straightened her shoulders and picked up another pup. Copper watched haughtily.

'You ought to go to bed and get some sleep, Steven,' Mark said, coming into the room for his coffee.

'I'm better here.' Steven said. He felt lazily comfortable, a state induced by the sedative the doctor had given him. His cold was no better, but he could cope with that. The intense misery and depression were over, and might have been part of another man. It was pleasant in the kitchen, where the fire had been built to a blaze. It was a huge room, warmed by the Aga at one end and the log fire at the other, and the couch was drawn across the angle of the chimney corner. Copper was stretched on the sheepskin rug, and Bob, clearly certain that life had turned completely upside down, lay beside the cat, and occasionally had a look at his puppies, as if aware that he was their father. Once he licked at one of the tiny dogs, but Bess growled, and he went away meekly.

One of the young soldiers came into the room.

'Looks like Christmas all over again on your churn table,' he said, and dumped several parcels on the table. 'There's loads of stuff out there. They're handing it over the gate.'

It was unbelievable. The grocer had sent a huge box full of both necessities and luxuries, with a note of condolence. There was a bottle of whisky from Herbert Green, pots of jam and marmalade from the Vicar's housekeeper, there were cakes from women in the village, and a stack of letters. Susan, looking at them, felt her eyes fill with tears again and ran off into the bathroom.

'What on earth's got into Sue?' Mark asked irritably. He hated howling women and Susan had never shown such symptoms before.

'They're all like that when they're in calf,' Joey said without thinking.

'Joey!' Sarah said reprovingly. She turned and saw Mark's astounded face. 'Didn't you know?'

Mark shook his head.

'And I'd like to know when she told you,' he said.

'She didn't. She's got that look about her. Always tell when a cow's in calf by her eyes. And the same with a woman.'

'You must be joking,' Mark said uncertainly.

'That's what I used to think, but he's always right,' Steven said. 'Congratulations,' he added, smiling.

Mark sat down and drained his coffee mug and held it out for more.

'I don't know what we'll do now,' he said. 'We're broke ... it's all very well to live from commission to commission with the two of us. But with a baby to keep ... I'm going to have to find a job.'

'Don't you go bothering Sue about that now,' Sarah said firmly. 'Time enough to worry later. You don't want her to lose the baby through worrying.'

Mark sat, staring at his boots. The future suddenly seemed terrifying. He had not wanted so much responsibility. You started out gaily enough, and then you got caught. He could see himself staid and settled, a nine to five commuter in some ghastly office all to provide home comforts for a child that he had never intended to have.

Steven was looking through the letters.

'A letter for Sue,' he said.

'For me?' Susan had returned, and was stroking Copper, her blonde hair cascading over her face.

She opened it, curious. The postman had known that she and Mark were at the farm and brought all their mail to them. The village knew everything, Susan thought. She began to read the letter and was so startled that she almost stopped breathing. All the colour went out of her face, and Sarah helped her into the big armchair.

'Sue!' Mark said, his voice anxious.

She held out the letter.

It was from Robbie, and for a moment the image of the little plump man, with his thin grey hair and sad pebble blue eyes, looked down at him, not as he had been the night before, but as he had been a week or two ago, when he had come to see them and sat for the whole of one evening, saying almost nothing, stroking Copper, and staring into the flames as if there he could find an answer to some vital question that always seemed to be on the tip of his tongue but that was never asked.

'He's left everything he had to Sue,' Mark said. 'He knew

119

what he was going to do, long before he did it. He had cancer. He didn't want to wait.'

'He's left me a fortune,' Sue said, her voice shaking almost as much as her hands. She looked into the fire. 'He's not sure how much. His father was rich ... a brewer, and he's never even touched most of the income, let alone the capital. And he's the only one of them left.'

'I can't believe it,' Mark said.

'Life's a queer thing.' Steven eased himself into a more comfortable position. He was feeling much better, and knew now that two nights before he had been ill, been, quite literally, out of his mind. He wondered how many other people who succumbed to impulse, would have seen more clearly in the light of day, and known that if they had taken the way they intended it would have been a fool's game. There was always a future, and his task was to build again.

Mark was looking at the letter again.

'Steven, would you take a partner?' he asked.

'A partner?' It was something Steven had never contemplated. He stroked Bess's patient head. She had not left him for more than a few brief moments, as if sure he needed her, and as if determined not to fail him. Poor Bess. And he'd almost deserted her. She would have pined of grief. If ever there was a one man dog, it was Bess. She heaved a deep sigh and settled herself more comfortably. Her pups nosed her.

'None of my children want Hollow End,' he said at last. 'I think a partner might be a very good idea. I'm feeling my age, and Joey and Sarah aren't youngsters ... but are you sure, Mark?'

Mark nodded.

'I've always wanted to farm,' he said. 'I've watched your cattle and your sheep and seen the calves and the lambs, and I've envied you. It's a good way of life. I could always buy up your share if you felt you wanted to give up.'

'An old man's dreams of the years behind ee,' Steven said musingly, a stray tag crossing his mind.

'And your darter's youngest darter to mind ee,' Susan said. 'Steven, would you really take us as partners?'

Steven nodded.

'We'll build again at Hollow End,' he said. 'A big milking herd, and more sheep. With you two to help me, knowing that you'll go on and keep the farm, it'll be worth doing. The other night I felt it was all useless. I was too old to start again and none of my family is interested in the farm. I was building for nothing; for strangers to come to Hollow End. But if you two really want to come in . . .'

'We do,' Mark said, and leaned over to complete the deal with a farmer's handshake.

Susan put her hand between them.

'It's my money,' she said demurely.

Mark drew back.

'Don't be silly,' she said laughing. 'It's yours too. I was just reminding you that I also have a say.'

'What are you going to call him,' Steven asked.

'Robbie. Robert Steven . . .' Susan looked up at him and suddenly blushed. 'How did you know?'

'Joey knew,' Mark said. 'He says he can always tell when a cow's in calf, and you had the same expression.'

'Honestly!' Susan said, and began to laugh.

'You can never keep a secret in Salem Hardacre,' Sarah said.

Steven was looking at his letters.

'I've been promised nine cows, three pigs, and two ewes and whatever offspring they might have,' he said in a bewildered voice. 'I don't even know one of the men. He says the cow is a thank offering, as he's been spared, and the area he lives in has been declared free. I can't believe it.'

It was a day for the suspension of belief. People sent presents and letters and flowers, they sent food, and they offered cattle. Some offered free beasts, others offered cheap beasts, and one letter made Steven grin.

'Some dealer thinks I was born yesterday,' he commented. 'He's offering me dud cattle at about five times the market price, and there's only one place for that one.'

He consigned the letter to the flames.

CHAPTER FIFTEEN

A YEAR later, as Steven took his cattle into the milking parlour, he found it hard to believe that, so short a time ago, he had been in despair. The cheerful thump of the machines, and the noise of beasts moving again, shifted the ghosts that haunted the empty fields and yards.

Joey and Sarah had moved into the Tilley's small cottage and Mark and Susan had theirs, so that there was more room for young Robbie. Steven, taking the cattle back again to the fields, saw Susan put him in his pram. Today was the anniversary of Robbie's death, and there were flowers, waiting in the hall, to go on his grave. It was strange to think that the little man had had the power to change life for all of them. Strange to think that a year ago, they had all been on the brink of disaster, the edge of despair, and none of them could forecast that life would be good again.

Joey had taught one of the calves to come to him for bread. The ghost of Shala was laid, and her picture hung in the kitchen, as Mark had drawn her. They could all remember her now with affection tinged with only a little regret.

There were lambs in the lambing shed, and bullocks in the far field. New heifers frisked in the meadow. Pigs grunted in the sties. Mark and Susan had invested wisely, and were learning fast. When the time came for Steven to give up he would go knowing that the farm he had built was in the best possible hands. He bent to pat the pup that they had kept from Bess's litter, and Bess, jealous, came to butt his hand.

'It's hard to think that only a year ago today we thought all this had ended,' Steven said, as he sat down at the breakfast table.

'At times it would be nice to know the future,' Susan said. 'If we'd only known we wouldn't have wasted all that worry and misery.'

'I suppose it should teach us that worry's a waste of time,' Steven said, cutting up bacon and eating avidly. He held out a piece to Bess, who had come to sit beside him. 'But we never learn.'

He looked through the window. The magpies had bred over the years. One of them flew up from the meadow. He remembered the magpie that had flown before the epidemic started.

'One for sorrow.' he said involuntarily.

Susan looked out of the window as a second magpie joined the first.

'Two for joy,' she corrected him, and looked out of the window at the pram where her son slept peacefully. Beyond him there were fields full of cattle. On the side of Eagle Hill the sheep grazed. Soon the second batch would be put in the lambing shed, and the first ewes and their lambs released in the field by the farm, where they could be watched carefully and guarded against snow and extreme cold.

Beyond Eagle Hill Ken Martin's matchless Jersey herd grazed unharmed, and Ken had given his own thanks by buying two cows and sending them to Steven with his and Mollie's love. The motorway had come to Jack Dodds' land, but he still bred his beagles and the pack ran again, and Steven often joined Ed Lucas and Mark as whipper in.

That night, when Steven sat on his log at the edge of the meadow, he looked up the hill and saw the moon shadow the ruined village, and wondered if among the unhappy creatures believed to haunt the gloom, Robbie too wandered. But he did not think so. Robbie had laid his own ghost to rest and found peace after a lifetime of misery.

The stone farmhouse loomed under the trees. Moonlight flirted on cow and sheep and floated serene on the water. Bess nosed her impatient muzzle into her master's hand. A cow lowed nearby.

There was a light in the lambing shed. Steven went to look at his sheep and found Joey kneeling beside a ewe that had just produced twins. He watched the two tiny beasts clamber to unsteady feet and the ewe nose them.

'Fine crop of lambs we'll have by spring,' Joey said, and Steven went to bed, his ghosts laid for ever, and lay listening to the sounds of movement outside, and the deep sigh in the night from the cows breathing beneath his window.

CHIA THE WILDCAT BY JOYCE STRANGER

Chia!

– the sound of the wildcat – as explosive as a gun-shot, as sharp as a slash of claws . . .

No tame and gentle fireside tabby, Chia is a prowling savage beast, who comes out of the night to kill. Often the only traces of her presence are stray feathers, blood-splattered bones and her terrifying wails in the night.

The wildcat has no friends but many enemies – the most feared of which is man. So Chia makes her home far from human haunts, where the looming shadow and the lethal gun of the hunter will not menace her kittens.

But even there the eagle and the fox give her no rest . . . and the wild cry rings out over the rolling glens –

Chia!

0 552 09891 4   70p

ZARA BY JOYCE STRANGER

Richard Proud coveted the golden-brown mare from the moment he saw her. Although he couldn't afford Zara, he bought her nevertheless, to breed him winners – foals that would restore the fortune of the Yorkshire stud where he bred and trained race-horses.

Zara was born a winner. She had to be raced and Richard Proud was determined that she should race; so despite personal crises – caused by his reckless wife – a snowstorm that isolated the stud only a few days before Zara was due to run, and an accident to her jockey, he had to find a way to let Zara prove her ability . . .

'Mrs Stranger's understanding of animals is sane and unsentimental, and her picture of the racing community is satisfying' – *Oxford Mail*

0 552 09892 2   80p

LOVE IN THE DOG HOUSE BY MOLLY DOUGLAS

Molly and Christopher Douglas discovered that everything could and did happen when they began to breed and board dogs on their Manitoba farm.

There were cockers, beagles, chihuahuas and Assorted others ... all kept in order by the Major, an elderly beagle of military bearing who kept strict discipline in the doggy ranks. There was Star, the toy terrier, who bullied the bull, and Twan Fu, the shih tzu, who arrived on a silver leash with day and night blankets, brush, comb, raincoat and choco drops, and had the time of his life rolling in cow pats and living like a real dog.

There were the people who came to buy and board, and dogs who were supposed to mate – and wouldn't. And above all there was the Douglas family, who turned their home into
THE DOG HOUSE ...

0 552 11333 6   85p

JUDITH BY ARITHA VAN HERK

Winner of the Seal $50,000 Canadian First Novel Award.

Judith the unanimous and enthusiastic choice of a panel of literary experts in London, New York and Toronto, a novel of rare power and refreshing originality, utterly unforgettable.

There were two Judiths:
the elegant city secretary trapped in a sordid affair with her boss – and the little country girl she'd once been, who knew as much about hog-raising as her Dad. And when Dad died, so did city Judith. The bitter girl who abandons her life and returns to her roots, is a loner, and intends to stay that way. A force to be reckoned with who can take on a pig farm single-handed – or a bar room full of angry men ... And when a man comes along who can reawake her passion, Judith's not ready to give up her independence.

Judith introduces an international audience to a major new Canadian talent, with a finely etched tale full of tenderness, fury, humour and sensuality, executed with a keen vision, warmth and brilliant characterisations.

0 552 11192 9   95p

A SELECTED LIST OF FINE
NOVELS THAT APPEAR IN CORGI

WHILE EVERY EFFORT IS MADE TO KEEP PRICES LOW, IT IS SOMETIMES NECESSARY TO INCREASE PRICES AT SHORT NOTICE. CORGI BOOKS RESERVE THE RIGHT TO SHOW AND CHARGE NEW RETAIL PRICES ON COVERS WHICH MAY DIFFER FROM THOSE ADVERTISED IN THE TEXT OR ELSEWHERE.

THE PRICES SHOWN BELOW WERE CORRECT AT THE TIME OF GOING TO PRESS (APRIL '80)

☐ 11202 X	The Tide of Life	Catherine Cookson	£1.50
☐ 11374 3	The Gambling Man	Catherine Cookson	£1.25
☐ 11368 9	The Fifteen Streets	Catherine Cookson	£1.00
☐ 11449 9	Maggie Rowan	Catherine Cookson	£1.25
☐ 11260 7	The Invitation	Catherine Cookson	95p
☐ 09074 3	Love and Mary Ann	Catherine Cookson	95p
☐ 09075 1	Life and Mary Ann	Catherine Cookson	95p
☐ 09076 X	Marriage and Mary Ann	Catherine Cookson	85p
☐ 11335 2	Katie Mulholland	Catherine Cookson	£1.50
☐ 08849 8	The Glass Virgin	Catherine Cookson	£1.25
☐ 11203 8	The Dwelling Place	Catherine Cookson	£1.25
☐ 09318 1	Feathers in the Fire	Catherine Cookson	£1.25
☐ 09373 4	Our Kate	Catherine Cookson	£1.00
☐ 11205 4	The Slow Awakening	Catherine Marchant	£1.00
☐ 11372 7	House of Men	Catherine Marchant	£1.00
☐ 11371 9	The Fen Tiger	Catherine Marchant	£1.00
☐ 10375 6	Csardas	Diane Pearson	£1.95
☐ 10249 0	Bride of Tancred	Diane Pearson	85p
☐ 10271 7	The Marigold Field	Diane Pearson	95p
☐ 10414 0	Sarah Whitman	Diane Pearson	£1.50
☐ 09462 5	Lakeland Vet	Joyce Stranger	70p
☐ 09891 4	Chia the Wild Cat	Joyce Stranger	70p
☐ 09893 0	Breed of Giants	Joyce Stranger	85p
☐ 09892 2	Zara	Joyce Stranger	80p

All these books are available at your bookshop or newsagent, or can be ordered direct from the publisher. Just tick the titles you want and fill in the form below.

CORGI BOOKS, Cash Sales Department, P.O. Box 11, Falmouth, Cornwall.

Please send cheque or postal order, no currency.

U.K. Please allow 30p for the first book, 15p for the second book and 12p for each additional book ordered to a maximum charge of £1.29.

B.F.P.O. & EIRE allow 30p for the first book, 15p for the second book plus 12p per copy for the next 7 books, thereafter 6p per book.

Overseas customers. Please allow 50p for the first book plus 15p per copy for each additional book.

NAME (Block letters) ....

ADDRESS ....

....